THE TIME OUTLAW

I0554577

S.R. Remus

THE TIME OUTLAW

FICTION4ALL

A FICTION4ALL PAPERBACK

© Copyright 2016
S.R. Remus

The right of S.R. Remus to be identified as author of this work has been asserted in accordance with the Copyright, Designs and Patents Act 1988

All Rights Reserved

No reproduction, copy or transmission of the publication may be made without written permission. No paragraph of this publication may be reproduced, copied or transmitted save with the written permission of the publisher, or in accordance with the provisions of the Copyright Act 1956 (as amended).

Any person who does any unauthorised act in relation to this publication may be liable to criminal prosecution and civil claims for damages.

ISBN 978-1-78695-9089

This Edition Published 2025
Fiction4All
www.fiction4all.com

Cover art by Deron Douglas

Special Thanks

"I want to write a book. I always have. I just never have. It seems difficult to write so much about something related to all the other stuff you've just written about."
"Write a book then if that's what you want." She said.
Thanks Jackie.

Dedication

At this point in time I would like to dedicate this
novel to myself, for writing it.
Go me.

Remember the
Old days,
Always,
Together, be
Alone
Never

Chapter 1

"I wish this didn't happen so much." Jensen James lay silently in his bed, struggling to wake up. *"This shit happened less often years ago when I drank all the time, but now, I just don't know. I wake up, and my head hurts. Why don't I remember much?"* Remaining silent, he shifts on the mattress. *"Oh my god, my fucking face, am I getting sick?"* Exhaling, caressing his face. *"My sinuses feel really congested, my cheeks are so sore."* Stretching and writhing in soreness, he smiles. *"I guess that means I had a hell of a night or at least I think I did. I feel like that was all just a dream. I'm not sure, but either way, I know where the medicine cabinet is."* Feet dragging along the floor, pushing off the bed, he pauses, letting his body stretch.

A king size bed, and an adjacent crude nightstand are crammed into his tiny, darkened room. The darkness hides the decaying, dilapidated walls. A floor lamp rests near the light switch. He struggles to find the switch. The room casts bleary light onto the unmade bed, hastily duct taped newspaper dangles over the window. Losing his hand on the wall, he traces the shoddy surface until he catches the switch. The room illuminates, Jensen rests his head on the wall; the glowing orange hue from the lamp reveals the unkempt bed, covered loosely by a sheet. The sun strains to break through the newspaper shackles binding it. The darkness of the walls gradually consumes the light as Jensen meanders toward the exit. His hand guides him toward the doorframe; remnants of peeling wallpaper and paint crumble at his touch.

Continuing out of the room to his right, the midnight, and dreary hallway keeps the light at bay, as if a cliff was trying to push the waters of the ocean aside, only to be driven back. Casually pulling himself around another doorframe, he enters the restroom. He fumbles about for the switch, knocking the brass plate loose. The bulbs flicker as the switch clicks to life, illuminating the room. Jensen glances into the cracked, shoddy mirror. Examining himself, he notices his blond hair matted to his head, caked in dirt, sweat and dried crimson flakes. Tirelessly, he carefully examines his slender jawline down each side, then trace back to his, sloping nose. Pausing, he stares at the flaky, dried blood, caked in streaks down his face.

"What the fuck happened to my face." He wonders. *"Maybe, I had a bloody nose? That would explain this, maybe it's my bad allergies."* He shakes his head. *"It can't be my allergies, there's too much blood."* He touches the flaky dried crimson streaks. He rubs his sore knuckle under the warm water, the soreness loosening in his fingers. Grimacing he unclenches his fists. *"I feel like a God damn geriatric, is this arthritis?"* *"I don't remember much of anything. My face looks swollen. I don't remember getting hit in the face."* Flush rosy splotches dot the landscape of his mouth, his cheeks, slightly enflamed, attempting to detract his focus from the large dark circle is developing around his left eye. *"I bet I got sucker punched, but*

by who?" He traces the circle, examining in wonderment.

Mind racing, he slides the mirror of the medicine cabinet revealing a large collection of pill bottles. He reads the labels tossing some to the side, and gradually gathering others in his hand. Bottles clink and clank, making their way into the trash, finally selecting a yellow bottle. *"hrngh"* Grunting, struggling to remove the cap, the pain in his hands has grows worse. The lid's seal pops, letting it fall to the floor he grabs two pills and tosses them in his mouth, throwing the bottle down into the sink. He swallows them, each pill scratching its way down his throat *"I've never needed a drink to wash them down before, why start now?"* *"I hope these do the trick."* Reading the label, he pauses. *"500 nanomites, eh I might need a fungal steroid injection tomorrow.* Running his hands through the water once more, splashing the water up against his face, the remaining dried blood loosens, streaming down, ensnaring the drain in its dastardly crimson hue.

Glaring back at him through his stone gray eyes, the mirror portals like a dimension into his soul, his pupils enlarged from the dim light. He pads the towel rack, but it's empty. He thrusts his other hand down into his hamper, retrieving a dirty, blood stained shirt out of his laundry basket and pats his face. Suddenly he drops the shirt, stepping back in a concerned horror. *"There's a lot of blood on here."*

Stern palpitations raise his heart into his larynx. *"I wonder what happened last night. I don't remember anything. It's probably nothing."*

Shaking his head in disbelief, he tosses the shirt back into the basket. His thoughts flounder as he tries to reassure himself that it is in fact nothing, yet he wonders. He flicks the light switch as he exits the bathroom towards the kitchen, where the windows are also draped in the chic duct taped newspaper.

The dark kitchen's light switch, missing its switch plate, hangs loosely to the left of the fridge. The bulb ignites, chasing the darkness from the room. A strange substance oozes its way across the floor, catching Jensen's attention. The light attempts to reflect off of it. *"What the fucking hell is this?"* Murmuring, he crouches down to his knee, reaching out to touch the substance with his fingertips. *"Oh, what the fuck is this?"* Examining the tips of his fingers trying to determine what exactly the strange goo is. Perplexed, he rises back to his feet.

"Where did this come from? Why is this in here? What happened in here? This wasn't here yesterday. What happened last night?" Thoughts flood his mind, heart pounding, trying to escape his chest; he fears what may be in the fridge.

"I need to look." Convincingly he extends his, arm, trembling immensely.

Inhaling deeply as he pulls on the handle, the sealed rubber stripping of the refrigerator pops as it begins to separate from the door and frame. Attempting to peer inside, he's interrupted by a loud, commanding knock at the door, halting his investigation abruptly. Jensen releases the door, the rubberized coating makes a soft sucking sound as it reseals to the frame. Cautiously he maneuvers through the dimly lit kitchen and into the living room. He traces his path lightly, knowing exactly where the furniture in the dark apartment is situated; he carefully heads to the door.

The front door, outlined by exterior light trying to force its way inside the dreary apartment, stands in front of him. Jensen peers out through the glass peephole, an outline of a man, a gregarious man, fills the fish-eyed frame. The sun's rays cast down over the man, rendering his features unnoticeable.

"What do you want?" Jensen's, hoarse voice deepens; he clears his throat, attempting a mild intimidation tactic.

"My name is Hector Luna. I was sent here to look after you Jensen. Someone wanted to make sure you're okay. We've been looking for you for a couple weeks." He responds, apathetic, in a veiled attempt to conceal the reason why he stands alone outside.

"Who? Look, I don't know you or anyone that would be concerned with my well-being." Jensen replied, his voice filling with concern.

"Jensen, just let me in. I need to make sure you're okay. You have a lot of people looking for you. I'm one of two people that don't want to see you get hurt. Just open the door for a minute so we can talk." Hector, impatient, calmly motions to the side, catching Jensen's attention.

"Why did you do that with your hand? Who are you motioning to?" He slinks back from the door, overwhelmed with mistrust. He retreats through the apartment, rushing his steps and avoid furniture in his path. His mind begins to fill with images of a tunnel, a pathway and a gorgeous red eyed woman smiling. Quickly it's replaced with the knowledge a hidden staircase underneath his bed. He tosses the mattress to the side, pushing on the bed. It lurches against the wooden floor, scratching the surface as he pushes with all of his might. He pushes it far enough to reveal the entrance to the secret staircase. *"Goddamn time rift memory floods."* Muttering as he tumbles down the stairway, crashing down onto the muddied tunnel floor below. More memories flood through his neurons; he shakes his head hoping to organize the information coming back to him. He pauses as a barrage of knocking echoes through the apartment. Sighing heavily, he proceeds down the creaking and moaning steps.

Two larger men burst through the door, crashing the wooden barrier to pieces. Their frames fill the doorway. Hector Luna walks in behind them, similar in build to the first two men, he barks out commands.

"Find him! I didn't hear or see him leave. He is in this apartment. Check everywhere!" He commands out to the others. Frantically, they search through the apartment. Chairs, sofas and small end tables fly through the air. The men make quick work of the living room, making a brief pause into the kitchenette before moving onward through the apartment. One of the men dives into the bathroom, thrashing about at the shower door, revealing no one. The other begins in the bedroom tossing the mattress set to the side. He begins kicking and smashing the bedframe until there is just a pile of broken, debilitated shards lying on the floor in front of him. He slides pieces out of the

12

way, revealing the scuffed floor, but he sees no staircase, no escape route, nothing. The other man joins him. "Closet." They state, nodding in agreement. Clothes and boxes fly from the closet outward across the bedroom floor. Rubbing their jaws while they browse through the mess they've created, they wait for Hector.

"Fuck!" He shouts. The loud echo of profanity reverberates through the building.

"James, Jeff, let's go, we've got to go make a phone call. I'm assuming he's not anywhere to be found right?" Hector continues to shout through the apartment. "Yeah, no sign of him, just like always." Jeff, the blonde haired one, responds. Jeff and James begin trudging their way back through the ransacked apartment, carelessly tossing and kicking anything out of their way.

"Where am I going? Who put those stairs there? Where does this tunnel lead to?" Jensen pants aloud as his legs pump feverishly, carrying him through the damp and muddied tunnel.

"Maybe I should have stayed, or maybe I can stop now. I can't trust them." He contemplates pausing, resting for a moment, but he convinces himself that this is one of those moments where if you stop, then you die. "What was in the fridge? Who were those guys? What the hell happened last night? Last night, more like what happened the last few weeks. Come to think of it, I can't remember the last month. I don't even know what today is or even where I was at. Well, I don't think I knew where I was at, but how did I know where those stairs were? Are they still after me? Those stairs should have been easily found. I need to keep running." He continues along. The ambience around him grows darker, colder. "Oh, man, where the fuck is this tunnel taking me? There's got to be a way out soon, it's getting cold." As he runs, he becomes alarmed at the gradually decreasing temperature, and where the tunnel may be leading.

"Is it winter right now?" Thoughts of the current season begin to course through his brain. "*It was warm in the apartment wasn't it? I didn't see snow around Hector, right, that was his name, Hector Luna. What is going on?"* Questions with no answers begin to overtake his thought process.

Just as miraculously as it had appeared, the tunnel begins to dissipate, fading into particulates of dust. Suddenly the muddied tunnel matriculates with gray slate walls streaking by him on either side. "Well this seems a little more reassuring." He mutters as the development of the tunnel seems to progress into a sound structure. He emerges through the mysterious particle cloud. The muddied ground solidifies under his feet.

"Concrete," he mutters, slowing to a brisk walk. His chest pounds as he gasps for air. An overwhelming familiarity strikes a chord deep inside him. He clutches his sides as he turns his focus upward. Bright lights reveal a massive door reaching skyward; it stands at least twenty feet high. He surveys the door continually looking over his shoulder back through the tunnel, but nothing seems to be clear on the other side of the particle encased fog.

14

"I hope I'm not stuck." He ponders as he turns back to the door, looking for a way to open it. A glowing red light hangs to the left massive door, it emits a digitized beeping noise before a loud clunk radiates through the space around Jensen. The light flashes yellow and then to green. Metallic screeching and egregious thuds echo as large latches release the door from its frame. The metal door moans as it opens. Bright lights shoot into the area around him. He squints, peering through the light. A clear path into a city alley rests in front of him. He steps into the alley way. Buildings reach towards the stratosphere. Hover cars zoom and whir, flying above him in the air, eluding other vehicles and ducking and diving in between buildings.

"I should be terrified." He thought, but the comforting familiarity within him makes this place feel like a home, his home.

"Why do I know this place?" He mutters, gradually moving forward through the alleyway, catching every new, yet familiar site and processing it. Jensen arches back looking upward into the sky. All the buildings reach into the skies above, the alleyway; all these things are seemingly familiar. He notices the dust particles from the fog begin subsiding from around him. Turning, he looks for the doorway, but it's gone. He scratches at his and begins walking quicker through the alley. He turns to his right and ends up on a busy thoroughfare. He carefully examines the advanced nature of his surroundings. Airlock doors, whooshing and swooshing as people enter and exit buildings are drowned out by the mystifying electronic sound of

human genetic teleport stations. Waiting lines of people, looking to teleport somewhere else fill the sidewalks outside of the skyscraper buildings. All this takes place beneath the chaotic scene taking place above, as the hover cars overrun the sky above. "When did… when were those invented?" He pauses, forcing himself to question what he's witnessing. "Where am I?" His mind struggles, but he presses on, navigating through the mysterious city.

Jensen strolls down the main street, cutting and turning to avoid bumping into any of the strange people dotting the sidewalks. They occasionally exchange casual glances with him. He slows approaching a sign that switches back and forth between different holographic displays.

"Welcome to Apace, home of the Latentech Corporation; the leader in scientific innovation." The sign transmits its preprogrammed electronic greeting. Jensen can't tell if it was directed at him or if it's a preprogrammed message. His mind boggles, jumbling a rushing flood of information.

"Apache," he mutters. "I'm home." He registers the current street, technological advancements, and surroundings with the place he grew up in. He notices a group of four sky-rise buildings tucked in the left corner of the intersection

Jensen rushes across the street, crossing rapidly not waiting for any kind of street signal, or even looking for any cars still using the roads beneath the bustling traffic ridden sky fare. He walks past a marble slab. An etched out bronze sign reads "The Apache Sky-Rise Quads." He moves quicker as the way home becomes eerily reminiscent, almost like he had never left. He presses along down the pathway between two of the buildings associated with the quads. He enters into the elaborate atrium that connects the four buildings of the quads. He passes by an old bent over willow tree. He pauses, crippled as an intense pain throbs in between his eyes. "Apartment 14D, Olivia," he whispers to himself. He rushes into one of the buildings, suddenly knowing exactly where he needs to go.

Chapter 2

A beautiful bouquet of cadmium orange lilies adorns the top of a silk black table. Four thin black leather chairs are neatly pushed under each side. The dining room runs straight through to the living room where it greets a black microfiber couch and matching chaise lounge angled awkwardly in the middle facing towards a grandiose swirl marble fireplace. A clear glass screen is mounted above the fireplace, currently displaying a live 3D projection of the current sporting events the small outline of an anchorman in the corner.

His new surroundings are vastly more luxurious than the previous apartment he had fled. Yet, as he continues his exploration of this luxurious new space, an eerie calmness comes over him. The sense of familiarity slowly brings more memories. He remembers the year and his mind finishes sorting his thoughts. He recollects the story of his life up to this point.

"I better look around a bit closer, just in case." His mind urges him to make sure he's alone and safe.

Jensen walks cautiously through the living room and down into the well-lit hallway. Paintings of desert sunsets line both sides of the hall. Halfway he passes by the kitchen, taking in the luxurious exuberance. Black marble floors contrast with the stainless steel futuristic looking appliances, promoting an air of elegance. He continues down the hall, pausing to look to at the restroom on his right. The tile matches the kitchen and the houses a grandiose, extravagant, clay stand-in shower. The large vanity mirror recessed into the wall reflects a mint green granite countertop gingerly supporting dual bowl sinks sitting on burgundy cabinets.

"That's a bit much." He mutters, turning to continue the tour of his apartment.

As he crosses the threshold of the bedroom, his eyes sweep the room. Much larger than the room he woke up, the walls are encased in gray. The black lacquer bed frame reflects a small amount of light, showcasing the wood. The holographic projector offers him a scrolling text - Video Port 1 is not detected." He attempts to check out the walk in closet but is blocked at the entrance by boxes of clothes and shoes stacked to the ceiling.

Jensen ponders the problem closet, turning and stepping back out into his bedroom. Overwhelmed he struggles to remember the finite details on how he has such nice things. He remembers most of his life now, but his head has begun to hurt again. It's becoming a familiar and unsettling effect.

"I need to rest." He thinks, scooting onto the cushioned bed. "This has been a long interesting day." He tries to put his mind at ease as he nestles in for the night lifting and pulling the comforter down tightly over his shoulder.

"I'll have more time to sort this entire mess out in the morning." Jensen takes a few deep breaths as his mind grows silent and his eyes drew to a close.

***

A well-dressed figure finishes speaking to a thunderous roar of applause. Jensen tosses and turns dreaming about this familiar man. The scene playing out in his mind and the speech constantly repeat in his mind, making sleep futile. Even in his dreams he can't seem to get a grasp on reality. His mind won't allow him to have one full night of sleep. Jensen's only able to briefly shut his mind off.

He struggles to open his eyes as his left eye fixates on a series of glowing, red numbers. He blinks his eyes again attempting to focus the blurring digits on the clock face. The time reads 520.

"What time did I start to lie down?" He wonders. He hadn't paid attention to the time when he crawled in bed. Sore and swollen, he begins to sweat with a mild fear. He rolls back toward the clock, covering his face with a spare pillow trying to force his way back to sleep. His mind keeps playing the same dreams and conversations over and over.

In his mind, he believes that someone wants to capture him. His mind drifts from the repetitive dreams and begins to reassure him that he knows more, he just needs more time to let it all come back.

"If only," he pauses thinks. "If I could just relax and get some rest. Maybe some food and a drink will settle me down." Rolling out of his bed, he tests his balance, still sore from the earlier tunnel sprints. His hands and face are beginning to writhe with pain and tightness,

"My medicine must have finally worn off. I knew 1000 milligrams wasn't enough, it never is." Angrily, he wonders if there's some medicine in this apartment. He saunters out of the bedroom toward the kitchen.

Without warning, a loud, commanding knock reverberates through the apartment.

"God damn it!" He whispers. He freezes in the hall, fear coursing through his body, wondering who knew he was here.

"Nobody knows I'm here, right? Maybe it's someone who can help me understand." As the seconds sneak by, another commanding knock echoes through the apartment, shaking him from his thoughts. His eyes wander through the luxurious, extravagant apartment, affixing solely on the enormous doors that stand between him and the unknown world. Uneasy, he feels that whoever is outside will not go away quickly. He contemplates answering or running

The metallic frame surrounding the large doors reflects into the expansive size of the living room as the contemporary black oak furniture allows for easy movement between the bookcase and the black leather sofa. The coffee table is centered squarely with the sofa, a few magazines tossed haphazardly on its surface. Sitting the sofa, he places his head into his hands. Another knock echoes through the apartment, the sound waves resonating down through his spine.

"Here we go again." He thinks, leaning back against the sofa. "These people are after me still? What have I done?" Frantically, he sorts through his memories and understand who could be at the door. Another knock, more frantic and less commanding caused Jensen to swallow the lump in the throat.

Reluctantly, Jensen rises from the couch and slowly approaches the large front doors. As he closes the distance a small pad extends out from a keypad on the right side. A young, fit, very attractive female displays upward of the holographic pad. Her hair is long, black, and stretches down her back. She looks to the left and right, as if someone is watching her. She wears a tight maroon leather suit, with brown, thick padded shoulder and chest pads and knee high black boots. He keeps his focusing on her face. Her soft olive skin is accentuated by her violet eyes. His gut instincts warn him to be cautious, even though she seems familiar.

A smaller keypad extends out towards Jensen. He reaches out and traces the keypad. "54896797." He mutters the numbers as he inputs the eight digit code.

"Olivia" Her name escapes his lips as the doors thud, and the female figure rushes through the open frame.

"You made it back! I'm so happy you made it back!" Smiling, she throws herself at Jensen embracing him passionately. Confused, rests his arms around her half-heartedly. She pulls away staring into his empty gray eyes.

What's the matter? You don't recognize me? You weren't gone to long this time. Did you experience a blood drain?" As she speaks, her voice puts him at ease.

"I, I'm not sure. You seem familiar to me, just like this apartment. Deep inside me, you are very familiar to me. I, I can't remember anything. One minute I'm in a rundown apartment, the next I'm being chased by a large man and his goons. Now, I'm being hugged by a beautiful woman in a beautiful apartment, apparently in a future. I don't even really know who or what I am."

Confused, Jensen slides by the woman reaching out at the keypad. His fingers dart across the keypad reentering the code on the keypad. The large locking beams latch from inside the door, the loud thud emanating from the latching echoes through the secure apartment.

"It's okay Jensen. These have been happening a lot lately." She gently slides her hand down his arm. Jensen's head snaps quickly downward, following her hand as it glides across his skin.

"You've just experienced another blood drain. I've been helping you recover from them. The more you've been time rifting, the worse and more frequent the blood drains have gotten. I'll get you caught up on everything. The quicker you are back to being yourself, the better off we will be." Jensen gradually relaxes, as his heartbeat and the feeling of his pulse in his throat slows.

"Tell me everything, I, but really confused and paranoid." She steps into him, wrapping him tightly in her strong muscular arms. Her embrace is strong but gentle as she holds onto Jensen.

"I'll start with the most important things and work my way back." She guides him to the couch.

"I'm Olivia Jima and luckily for you, I am your girlfriend. You, Jensen, are a member of a rebel group, known as the Awakened. Your father, Ambrose, is after you. Ambrose is in the business of sending people back into the past, to alter the future, so that he can take advantage of bets or regulatory changes to make money or gain increasing political power. You learned about his plans when you were a teenager. Ever since, we have dedicated our lives to stopping him. Unfortunately, as we have succeeded in some events, your father has succeeded in others. Those men who you encountered during your last jump are known as Time Warp Sheriffs. They are part of a mercenary team able to be hired out from the Department of Time Justice, the regulatory commission on time warping. Sadly, your father and his political backing, not to mention the astounding amounts of money, have allowed him to corrupt the Apache government." Jensen squeezes her hand.

"So, why don't I remember anything, any part of any of this? Some of this seems familiar, even you, you seem familiar." He struggles as he questions her.

"Relax." She rubs his shoulder, attempting to remove the tension. "I'm going to get there." She puts her hand on his leg and smiles as he tries to relax the tension.

"Your memory loss, is directly associated with the act of a time rifting or warping. These two are very similar but a warp places you into that time period for a longer amount of time whereas a rift, is a more accurate travel to a specific moment in time. This allows you to potentially jump to an exact moment to stop an event from occurring. Either way, the frequency with which we have had to rift or warp has increased dramatically since we're being hunted. The blood drain and memory loss is your body's reaction to the strain. It's also the way your brain erase memories that you were the one that went back in time to stop or change." Jensen stares at her fully enthralled by all of this.

"I know this is a lot to take in, but we've got to get you back to normal and your fathers goons won't be far behind. You're going to have to move and get caught up. The typical side effects last two or three days. However, with our newfound steroid you'll be back to yourself in the morning." Her hand slides into her chest plate, removing a small, dark blue bottle.

The bottle is no larger than the length of his knuckle to his fingertip; the liquid inside the bottle is nearly gone. The metallic silver cap sits secured to the bottle's neck with a small silver chain. Jensen twists the cap off.

"How much do I need to take?" He asks, guiding the bottle to his lips.

"Just a drop, it's a highly concentrated Centella (Sinhala) extract from the past. Highly illegal in our time, so years ago we rifted back and brought a wealth of plants into a hidden greenhouse. Sadly, most of it was found and destroyed. That bottle is all that remains; the rest was burned into extinction." Her voice calms him.

He tries to remember why he would have turned against his father. Deep inside, he feels a passion begin to yearn again. He tilts the bottle and lets a drop of Centella fall on his tongue. He sits back on the couch and looks at Olivia as she snuggles he head on his chest. "So we are being chased by bad guys? What do we do now?" His arms tighten around Olivia as he drifts off, thinking about their plans.

Chapter 3

A woman with olive skin lies sleeping under her covers, exposed from the shoulders up. The alarm besides her bed screeches and she opens both eyes. She yawns and stretches luxuriously as she turns off the intruding alarm. As she rolls out of her bed she adjusts the strap of her bra and casually tosses the sheet aside. She goes to the large glass window overlooking the city, her muscles flexing as she moves.

She stops dead center of the glass door looking out. Across the street, a group of young teenage boys, dressed up in navy blue blazers, white collared shirts with white ties, tucked neatly into pressed tan slacks. They all stare, gazing up in adoration at beautiful woman, looking down over them.

"I'm so in love with you Maria!" They all laugh and join in shouting, confessing their love to her. She laughs knows she provides undying fantasies for all the boys before they head to school. She gently presses her hand to her lips, to blow a kiss out through the door to her fan club below. Turning two steps back into her bedroom, she reaches behind her back unfastening her brassiere, tossing it at the door, hitting the glass door gently before falling to the floor. A roar of whooping and cheering erupts from the watching boys below. She smiles, giggling as she walks to her washroom.

The water from the shower trickles down her body, coursing like a smooth stream across her body before it splashes into the basin of the shower. She reaches down to turn off the water pausing letting the remaining drops trickle off her body before she wraps herself in a towel. She fits it snugly across her bosom, the towel hugging her curves. She stands in front of the small oval mirror over an ivory pedestal sink. She examines her face in the reflection, as she pulls her black leather make-up pouch from vanity wire rack storage bin tucked below the sink. She tugs at the zipper, revealing a cascading selection of different colored lipsticks, eye shadows and various other make-up products. She selects a bright fire red gloss lipstick and traces her lips. She pauses to blow a kiss at the reflection in the mirror. As she finishes, a faint ring fills the silence.

Maria hurriedly tosses her makeup back into the leather bag and it into the wire rack bin. She sprints out of the bathroom, and sits on the edge of her bed, crossing her legs. She grabs a nearby headset and places it over her still damp black hair.

"This is Maria, how may I help you?" She answers in a soft, friendly undertone.

"Maria," the voice on the other side is firm and masculine. "How are you my dearest?" Excited by the caller, a smile spreads across her face.

"Hello Ambrose! It's so nice to hear your voice, I was just thinking about you." Her tone is slightly higher now.

"That's good, that's great really! I was thinking about you too. What are you up to today? I would like to see you; we have some stuff we have to discuss. It's sort of urgent." The firmness in Ambrose's voice softens hearing her excitement.

"Well, I just got out of the shower, was going to get dressed and wait around for you to call, but it looks like you already did." She flirts, biting her lip as thoughts of Ambrose cross her mind. He chuckles through the transmitted connection.

"How long will it take you to get ready dear, are you already dressed?" He inquires. "Well, if you consider me in just a towel dressed, then I'm ready whenever you are." She bites her lip, running her hand down her body. She falls back onto the bed, the towel unwrapping. She lies there naked, staring into the ceiling.

"Do you know what I'd like to do to you right now?" Ambrose teases. Maria's temperature rises. She runs her hands down her chest groping her breasts in each hand, her fingers massage her erect nipples. She arches her back as her hand slides down in between her legs.

"Mmm, what would like to do to me?" She replies softly, anticipating his response.

"I'd like to," a phone rings in the background behind Ambrose. "I have to get this. My driver is downstairs already. Hurry up and get dressed, we have something we need to discuss." He disconnects the phone call quickly. Maria lays, stunned and frustrated with the quick turn of events. "Ugh, men," She takes the headset off and tosses it across the room.

Maria walks quickly out of her apartment. She turns and swipes her yellow keycard through the card reader. She walks down the hallway, in her black tall leather boots, tight black leggings and a deep v-cut t-shirt, showing the tops of her breasts. A short, red jacket with brown padding at the elbows and shoulders cover her shoulders, and little else, unable to button across her breasts. The neckline sits loose along her shoulders direct attention toward her chest. She walks with more precision than a runway supermodel.

Maria exits the elevator and emerges through the front doors of the apartment building. Waiting outside is a navy blue, ovular shaped, hover car, accentuated by a grill, side mirrors and thin trim along the bottom of the car, encased in bright reflective chrome, reflecting the sun into her eyes as she approaches. A door slides open revealing a luxurious white leather bench seat, a small wooden table sits in the middle of the hover car. She slides in, ducking her head to avoid the plush interior roof. She positions herself square with the small table and looks around the inside.

"This is the life I deserve," she thinks as the door slides shut, locking with a faint *click*. Maria relaxes into the seat. Her eyes catch a small pure white envelope sitting in direct center of the small table. She leans forward, picking up the envelope, the faint hint of a soothing rose, reaching her nose, She smiles, sliding her finger gently down a small opening in the envelope. She pulls out a small piece of paper, scribbled in elegant cursive writing,

I'm so thankful for you, the woman of my dreams.

Here's to me always being your dream.
Love eternally yours,
Ambrose.

30

She beams brightly with a loud sigh placing it gently against her chest. She stares off into the ceiling, lost in her thoughts.

The hover car zips along weaving in and out of traffic. To the naked eye it appears to be on a direct line toward the enormous Time Justice building that casts its shadow over Apache. Maria sits forward, glancing out the right side window. The city of Apache zips by in a blur. Other hover cars seem stationary as hers speeds along. The car pays no attention to the people walking or surrounding traffic. The Time Justice building grows massive in the windshield. Her anticipation is palpable as she slides closer to the door as the hover car gradually slows. The car slides into position, elevating higher off the ground and parks parallel to the curb. The door slides open and she ducks out of the car, adjusting her jacket and pulling the tops of her boots back to just underneath her knees.

The Department of Time Justice looms large above Maria. Thousands of large windows stretch upward with large white panels dividing each row of glass planes, identifying the many floors. Atop the massive structure sits a large, clear glass globe, the highest point in Apache, overlooking the vast stretches of the city. Maria walks toward two small doors guarded by two massive figures, adorned in all black robotic like armor holding large rifles across their chests.

"You'll be sorry!" A small young boy runs haphazardly towards the doors, bumping carelessly into her. He pauses grabbing a small rock from his left pocket and quickly tosses it towards one of the robotic like figures. The rock hits one square in the helmet with a light smack. A less intimidating female figure dressed in an all blue suit, with a small gold badge on her right breast pocket tackles the young boy, hitting the ground with a loud thud. The female figure wrestles to grab the young boy's hands. Maria picks up her pace and approaches the scuffle, making out the small Time Justice emblem on the female's left sleeve.

"Help me miss!" The young boy shouts. She glares deeply into his eyes; scowling as she raises her right foot and strikes her boot squarely between the eyes on the bridge of his nose, The boy stops moving, his eyes and nose flowing blood where her boot struck him. The female that had been wrestling with the young boy ties his hands together and stands, looking at her.

"You're welcome cadet. I suggest some more practice with your apprehension techniques is in order." She says, condescendingly as she proceeds into the Department of Time Justice.

Inside the Department slick granite floors stretch between the glass walls. A solitary, circular, black marble counter sits directly in the middle of the building. An old woman, with her hair curling upwards with tinges of blue strands hanging carefully down either side of her face, greets Maria as she approaches.

"Good morning my dearest, Mr. Ambrose is expecting you; you can go right on up." Ignoring the old woman, she proceeds to a flat black section of flooring at the very back of the building. A short, square glass wall rises from the floor around her.

What floor? A mechanical voice arises from the floor that she stands on.

"The Orb," Maria replies calmly.

Fifty-four? The mechanical voice asks. Frustrated, Maria repeats her request.

I'm sorry, did you say Fifth floor? The voice from the floor asks again.

Maria angrily stomps her foot on the floor. *"Mother fucker, I said THE ORB!"* She shouts; her voice carrying across the room. The old woman at the desk turns to look at her.

Proceeding to the Orb, please have your key card ready to swipe into the room. The robotic tone from the speaker replies. *Please stand away from the edge, time to Orb is two minutes. Thank you.*

The mechanical voice clicks off as the black floor tile rises, stopping waist length of Maria. The black flooring wobbles as it disconnects from the docking station. A section of the floor slide quickly and smoothly out of the way and Maria gets on. The lift continues upward, performing a puzzling choreographed dance as Maria makes her way floor by floor waiting patiently to get to the orb.

The black flooring Maria is riding now approaches the bottom the Orb. It's secured to the ceiling to the 90th floor of the Time Justice building. Long, sleek metal struts shoot from all around the bottom of the Orb to the four corners of the building below. Securing each of the metal struts to one another are more thick paned glass, providing a clear view stretching out beyond the Apache horizon, occasionally dotted with the shadows of smaller buildings offsetting the skyline.

Maria steps forward as the lift comes to a stop. A small metal rod protrudes from the bottom, extending to a stop in front of Maria. She removes a small red key card from her left front pocket, and inserts it into a small metal box. The metal box emits a faint *beep* and slides up the metal rod rotating back towards the Orb. The bottom of the Orb glides open, narrowly avoiding the metal struts connected to the bottom. The flooring that Maria stands on casually rises through the opening. A loud *thud* brings the lift to a sudden halt. Maria survey the open glass walls of the Orb; gradually they come to a stop, highlighting a male figure leaning against a hefty polished wood desk. She descends and walks towards him.

"Hello, my beautiful princess," the voice greets Maria. She smiles, beaming back at the figure. "Ambrose, you tease me again like you did on the phone and I will make sure I get exactly what I want," she replies coyly.

Ambrose straightens, his clean-cut smile beams across his smooth shaven face. Maria's eyes trace his well-fitted suit, their heads tilting casually as their lips press together, kissing briefly. Ambrose gazes longingly at her, the silence thickens between them.

"So, what brings me here? Did you just miss me?" Maria purred.

"No my dear, unfortunately we need to discuss the business side of our relationship. I just spoke to Hector and he has once again had the most unsettling news for me." Ambrose's demeanor grew with disgust. Maria's smile faded

"I knew this day would come," she thought.

"What do you need me to do? What is the news? You know I will do anything you ask of me." Maria replied confidently. Ambrose walks to the other side of his desk. He pushes a manila folder back across the surface towards Maria

"It's Jensen," he said.

"Jensen? What about Jensen, did Hector get him?" Ambrose raises his hand; and Maria goes silent.

"He's back in Apache. Hector and his team chased him back here. We had tracked him to a specific point in time and they attempted to capture him again. According to Hector, Jensen time warped back here and supposedly is showing little to no signs of effects the blood drains typically have." Maria heard the worry in his voice and reached for the folder, skimming the contents, pausing as she came across a black and white photo of Jensen, the word WANTED stamped in red ink.

The paper read; *Jensen James is wanted for crimes against the people of Apache. He is considered armed and dangerous. Do not approach him. Please report sightings of him to the Department of Time Justice. If you possess the capabilities to permanently remove this threat from Apache; do so immediately and with caution. There is an immense reward for his death. DO NOT CAPTURE.*

"You, you want him dead now?" Maria inquires through the lump in her throat. Ambrose taps his fingers across his desk.

"You remember the details of our agreement, we both never thought this day would come, but Jensen's threat against me and all I have worked for has come." Ambrose turns to the windows looking across Apace.

"I will do anything Ambrose." Maria replies confidently, brushing away the discomfort in her chest.

Without facing her, Ambrose dismisses her with a wave of his hand. "That will be all dear. Take care." Maria retreats towards the section of flooring, stands as the small glass wall rises from the floor; stopping just short of her waist. She catches Ambrose turning his head to catch a final glimpse of her.

"He's dead to us Ambrose!" Maria says firmly, her voice carries through the tense air of the Orb. Slowly the glass doors below the tiled lift slide open and Maria descends back to the depths of the Department of Time Justice.

Chapter 4

"Yes sir, I understand you aren't happy. Something spooked him. We didn't do anything to tip him off that he was somebody else. These situations are very delicate, it's almost like the blood drain effect didn't cause him to forget anything. We're going to have to come back and track him again. Someone has to be aiding him; we know there are only two or three time outlaws who have ever been able to recover memories from blood drains. We may need to pay those criminals a visit upon our return." Hector spoke, confidently. He knew he was giving Jensen James more credit than the well-dressed, suited figure on the other side of the hologram wanted him to have.

"Look, Hector, my friend. Jensen James is an outlaw, a criminal. You and I have never been outsmarted by a criminal. Do I need to give you more help to capture him? Are you incapable of completing this assignment? This man, Jensen James, is starting to become looked up to by the citizens of the New World here in Apache. I gave you this assignment because I heard you and your team were the best. Is this not an accurate assessment?" The imposing tall figure with salt and pepper hair on the other end was wearing a black suit and tie. His piercing eyes narrowed in on Hector, only his voice betrayed his lack of confidence, projecting his stress and worry onto Hector.

"Mr. James, I understand your concern, my team is the best in the New World, Apache and we're easily the best in the department. There is no payment until you are satisfied with our service. I merely underestimated your son based on the information you gave me. I assumed he was a radical wannabe, trying to live up to the glory of the old time outlaws whom I've defeated. I know I need to bring out the big guns now and I also need access to prison cells 165103 and 262465. I need to interrogate some prisoners about blood drains. It appears we don't know as much as they do after all." Hector replied reassuringly.

"Hector, you have all the access you need. He is scum and is a wannabe; ever since he was little, that bastard shirked his responsibilities. I will not be made a fool of. Next time you have the chance, I give you authorization to commence and carryout kill order #5647, Jensen James, rebel time outlaw. I want his lifeless body paraded through the streets of the New World and his body displayed in Apache. Do you understand me Hector?" Mr. James shouted into the holographic communicator at Hector, who caught off guard at Mr. James' rage, simply moved the communicator away a few feet.

"Yes sir, I understand, we're on our way back. We will sign out the appropriate weapons for kill order #5647. Jensen James, son of Ambrose James, will not survive the end of the day." Hector terminated the hologram before Ambrose could continue his rant.

"Well gentleman, looks like our potential payday has increased, we've got a kill order for Jensen James. Let's go have a drink when we get back." Jeff, James and Henry all high five one another, smiles and laughter abound. They gradually pile into a nearby blue van, Department of Time Justice, emblazoned in gold etching along either side. Hector beams, knowing that a kill order brings up to four times the profit from the payer and the Department of Time Justice pays high dividends to the teams that execute kill orders.

Hector, Henry, Jeff and James remove thick, triangular, metal plates from the back of the navy blue van. Each plate is around four inches thick and made from extremely dense tungsten metal. The twins, Jeff and James along with Hector carry the plates with ease and place them behind the car. Henry, the smallest and weakest of the bunch slides his carefully onto his shoulder.

"Ugh, with as advanced as we are with holograms, why can't they make the telepad any lighter?" Henry exclaims; straining as he struggles with the weight of the plate. He changes position and tugs on the plate, dragging it along the trunk; he lets it drop to the ground. The plate smacks with a *thud* onto the asphalt of the parking lot, chipping in parts, the recoil from the plates resonates through his forearms. Henry continues to drag his plate, and then pushes his plate in between the other three members of his team. The others carefully set their pieces down and then slide their pieces together forming a large circle, six feet in diameter. Henry removes four cards and presses each one into a slot on each triangular piece.

"Henry, we're going to take your Texan ass to the gym for the next month. All those stories about Texans, and we get the last and weakest one in history." James cracks loudly, making everyone but Henry laughs.

"Yea, yea, well let's just get back first; we know if I didn't set this up we could end up being chased by soldiers in 1942, or dinosaurs thanks to you jackasses." Henry retorted, bring up some bad warp jumps by the twins.

"Calm down, everyone, Henry, I know you'll get us back safe like always." Hector interjects, restoring some of Henry's confidence and getting his crew back under control. Hector watches as Henry fusses about with a piece of holographic glass, inputting numbers into a small 3-d field. 1230, 06 January, 2013. Henry double checks his watch. If Henry is off by even a second into the future, the crew will end up disintegrating in the warp jump and Jensen James will elude his father once again. Hector, Jeff and James double, then triple check the numbers.

"Alright Henry, jump time is confirmed, hit it." Hector instructs Henry. Henry fusses around with his holographic glass for another few seconds.

"Warp is activated, jumping in three, two, and one." Henry counts, and with a press of his holographic screen, the four figures vanish. Appearing to stretch tall and wide, and then without a sound, the plate and the team are no longer standing in the parking lot. All that remains is the small chip in the asphalt where Henry had dropped his portion of the time warp plate.

Hector steps off the telepad, calmly surveying their arrival point in modern Apache. Seconds later, his handheld holographic communication unit buzzes with the name of "Ambrose Jones."

"Christ, what could this asshole want now? He can't even give me time to get prepared to go after the man he wants me to capture." Hector reluctantly he presses *accept* on the device. A three-dimensional figure of Ambrose appears, standing three inches tall off the face of the tool wrapped tightly to his wrist.

"Hector. I have more news for you. We know Jensen is back, Maria has the details of his address. I need you to meet her at the location I transmit to you at 1730. She has specific instructions on what to do in order to capture Jensen. Be prepared for a long night casing the place while Maria works on the inside. With all hope, she gets him subdued for you to bring him in, if not, your team will be outside to capture him when he walks or runs out of the door." Ambrose's arrogance emanated from the holographic image. Hector paused gathering his thoughts.

"Ambrose, we will be there. I wish you would let my team do the work you hired us for, but you're the boss on this contract, we'll do anything you ask of us for money. I need access to those prisoners' cells." Hector quickly changed the subject, hiding his hurt pride.

"Hector, my friend. You have access. I told the Control Warden that I had a good friend and his interrogative team coming by to ask those prisoners some questions. The prisoners will be primed and ready to talk to you about anything. I've got to go, my friend. I have a city to run. Oh, and Hector,

41

don't fuck this up again." Hector watched the little holographic man disappear.

"That guy is a huge asshole boss." Henry spoke quietly. He had snuck up on Hector. Hector jumped a little, and then slowly turned towards him. Hector forced a small smile; he knew Henry could tell he was upset with Ambrose.

"Henry, get the twins ready. We have to go visit some prisoners. We are going to learn a lot more about warp jumps and side effects from some of the most prestigious minds in Apache. Be ready to take notes." Hector spoke casually.

"Oh, I've got you Hector. I'll get everything prepared." Henry replied as he scurried off to gather the twins and their stuff. Hector watched him leave.

"*I like that kid, he works hard and I can always rely on his mental acuity.*" Hector thought highly of Henry, like a son he had never gotten to have.

He turned back to watch the bustling streets of Apache, as the hover van, equipped with emergency warning light and sirens; weaved in and out of traffic causing inquiring glances. Inside the van the twins and Henry joked around about Ambrose and tried to make light that this current customer, so readily and easily disrespected their boss. Hector, struggled to maintain his focus his mind racing with thoughts of disgust towards Ambrose. He had two prisoners to interrogate. His mission was to learn how Jensen was so easily able to recover from the debilitating side effects of time travel.

Why do we need telepads and all this equipment? Why do we have to have full medical teams? These were just a couple of the questions

Hector knew he would have to ask at the upcoming interrogation.

The hover van now coursed above an old two lane road, remnants of the past methods of travel. Dust and small rocks kicked into the air as the van wound its way carefully along the dilapidated path, hovering mere inches above the cracked and jagged asphalt, dotted with the occasional bush and tree. Outside of Apache the world seems deserted. Not a single sign of life could be traced over the growing, deserted, emptiness of life outside the city. The van slowed, making a smooth right turn, heading to a fortress.

Towering walls caked in a drab and cracking gray formed a massive square barrier. Thin razor wire ran along the top. Hector glanced at the green sign that read *Apache Maximum Security Facility, No Entrance,* followed by numerous smaller yellow signs warning visitors to turn around. The hover van comes to a stop as all four men look through the windows, waiting for the door to open. They are outside of two massive metal doors, chains and large beams seemingly affixed to keep anyone outside out and anyone inside; in. As the doors open, Henry and the twins turn towards Hector.

"Gentleman, let the fun begin." Hector said, sliding out of the hover van to the big metal doors of the facility. Henry and the twins follow, stretching as they keep pace with Hector.

Hector stands patiently in front of the massive doors. The twins and Henry flank him, behind the three's massive muscular frames. A small slit slides open in the middle of one of the doors, red mechanical eyes glare out, locking onto Hector.

"No visitors allowed," the mechanical voice droned. Hector stared back into the red eyes.

"My name is Hector Luna, I was sent here from Ambrose James. We have two prisoners to interrogate. I was told you would have the prisoners ready for us. We don't have time. We need to begin the interrogations immediately." He brusquely responds.

"What prisoners? We don't house prisoners. We kill them." The red eyes sized them up, its voice even more mechanical and emotionless than before. Hector paused, and then spoke.

"There are two prisoners here. Prisoner numbers are 165103 and 262465. They better already be in the interrogation cell. If this isn't prepared my boss, Ambrose James, will be sure to hear about the problems you're giving me. This is of the utmost importance. Let us in." His voice brimmed with authority and after a moment, the red eyes blinked. Slowly, loud metal *clanking* emanated from the massive doors. The red eyes disappeared from the door as one of the massive doors shifted inwardly creaking loudly, as if the door had not moved in decades, begging for some sort of reprieve from the dried, unlubricated metal on metal contact. The door halted with 18 inches of clearance.

"After you gentlemen, looks like a tight squeeze." Hector gestured toward the twins with a smile.

The twins slid in horizontally through the tight opening, their muscles inhibiting them. Henry slid in quickly with his small frame. Hector follows his large frame tight through the small opening. The four stand in a small courtyard, facing red eyed female about 10 feet away. She is small in stature, maybe Henry's height and just as scrawny.

"Right this way Mr. Luna, we have prisoner 165103 ready for you. You're going to have to interrogate them one at a time. We can't run the risk of them being in the same room together. You know, they were husband and wife at one time? It's such a shame what crime can do to such a beautiful woman. Prisoner 165103 has proven to be a little hostile as well, so we will let your team stay in the interrogating room with you. You look like you could handle yourself but we can't run that risk with the security." Her voice was soft and welcoming. Hector nods and turns toward his team.

"That will do just fine. His will be the short interrogation. Well, let's get to it." All five enter the main facility building.

Hector and the twins enter a small room with a silver metallic table and a tattered black chair pushed in neatly underneath, in the middle. The twins stand near the door as Hector moves forward, taking the seat. He drums his fingers as they wait for prisoner 165103. The small female walks in, guiding a sickly looking male to the other side of the table, his head covered by a musty burlap bag, tied tightly around his neck. The female turned to Hector, their eyes meeting. "Are you ready for this?" she chuckled.

Hector, taken aback, simply nods. Brandishing a knife and slicing the string, pulls off the burlap sack and the man lets out a horrific moan.

Hector stares at the figure, whose facial features resemble his own except for the black stiches cross crossing his lips.

"He can't speak." The red eyed female tosses a notepad and pen onto the table. She smiles at Hector, then turns, walking by the twins as she exits the room.

Hector leans forward in his chair. His eyes lock with the sickly figures as they stare each other down.

"This is how this is going to work. I'm going to ask you a series of questions. You, prisoner 165103, are going to write your responses on the notepad. If you don't comply, my associates are going to help you out." Hector gestures at the twins. The twins smile at the sickly figure and then flex their massive muscles, intimidating the scrawny male. Hector pushes a notepad and pen across the table.

"Do you understand?" The sickly figure looks at the twins and then back at Hector. He hangs his head, nodding at Hector's question.

"Good, good. This will be quick. First, what is your name prisoner 165103?" The male grabs the pen and carefully scribbles on the notepad; sliding it across the table. Hector looks down.

"I am Hector Luna, who are you?" Hector sits, stunned.

"You are not Hector Luna. I'm Hector Luna. If you're going to play games with me I will walk out of this room and leave you alone with my boys."

Hector leaned forward placing his elbows on the table, resting his chin on his clinched fists.

"Ungh!" The male lets out another high pitched sickening moan, as if screaming at Hector. Hector sighs.

"Boys; this prisoner is a waste of my time. I'm going to go see about getting the next prisoner interrogated. I can handle the next one on my own. Why don't you introduce our new friend here into your world of physical fitness? I'm sure he will welcome the activity." Hector stands and walks calmly by the twins. Jeff turns and shuts the door. He smiles at James.

On the other side of the door Hector hears loud sickening thuds and high pitched shrills from prisoner 165103. He heads down the hall, towards the next interrogation room.

The red eyed female stood outside a room as he approached.

"She's ready for you. She should be a little more compliant than the first one. Not as neurotic or sickly." She smiles, walking hurriedly back towards the shrieks coming from the other interrogation room.

Hector walks into the room, gently shutting the door behind him. The room is setup exactly like the first. He takes a seat across from a woman, maybe in her 40s with long black hair. Her head is hung low, keeping her eyes from looking at Hector. Hector glances over her, her skin looks soft and well taken care of, and smooth, very feminine.

"You understand how this works? I'm going to ask you some questions and I need you to answer them truthfully or you will end up like prisoner 165103. Trust me, that isn't something you want." Hector speaks softly, clearly frightened by his presence. She raises her head slowly and their eyes meet.

"Edm…" Hector raises his hand.

"Not here, Annalise. I have something important to tell you. Jensen James has returned. Ambrose has my team running all over Apache trying to capture him. We're supposed to be on our way shortly to attempt to make a grab again. This one will be harder to throw. Ambrose has Maria on his side; she's going to try to take Jensen to him in the morning. I had to come see you and let you know that everything was going as planned." Hector hurriedly tells her.

"It's so nice to see you again. I have never felt safer. Although, I was worried about, you know how being in here with me. The caretaker you assigned has been such a big help in keeping our plan a secret. I miss you. I hope we help Jensen and all the others of the resistance. This is such a trying time. We should make this quick." She replied. Hector returns the smile, switches back to interrogating Annalise as Henry enters the room

"Well Mrs. Jima. I'm sorry about your husband, but he was being uncooperative. I'm sure you understand. Your information will provide valuable in the arrest and most likely the death of Jensen James. You have done the denizens of Apache a great service." Hector finishes his spiel and walks out the door to Henry.

48

"Everything good boss, she spilled the beans quickly, eh?" Henry inquired.

"Yes Henry. You know how it is. I've always had a way with women. Her being a prisoner doesn't change that." Hector smiles, patting Henry on the back. Henry and Hector walk down the hall; the twins stand outside the first interrogating room.

"I'm going to have to clean that mess up." The red eyed female admonished Hector.

"Yeah, sorry about that, we have to be going rather quickly though. We have an elusive time bandit to capture. Rumors are he's back, but now we have the information needed to make sure he doesn't escape again." Hector motions his team out the door.

"I never did catch your name, surely I should tell Ambrose of how helpful you have been." Hector turns looking directly into the female's glaring red eyes. She looks past Hector as the door the courtyard closes behind Henry. She stands alone, face to face with Hector.

"I'm glad you came to see us again, Dad. Mom and I are doing well; we're excited that Jensen is back. Everything has been getting bad in Apache. I stay away from there just like you told me. It will be better around here with Hector gone. He was getting out of control." She looked up at his eyes. Hector/Edmund looked down at her smiling.

"I love you Olivia, we'll be able to live as a family again once Ambrose is taken care of." Hector turns to look down the hallway.

"Anna, you're still just as beautiful as you were on our wedding day." His voice carries to Annalise, who stands in the doorway of the second interrogating room.

"Be safe Edmund, I love you." Her voice tender, she turns away from the two figures. Edmund looks at Olive, he hugs her quickly.

"Time to go princess, I'll see you soon." Hector abruptly turns and leaves through the courtyard, catching up with Henry at the massive doors.

"Is everything alright in there, Hector?" Henry asks.

"Let's go catch a bad guy Henry." Hector replies.

The two slide out through the massive doors to the waiting hover van to return to Apache.

Chapter 5

"Jensen!" A voice echoes through a young man's bedroom.

"I'm sleeping." Jensen mumbles.

"Jensen Ambrose James, you are not going to be late for another day at the Apache Academy! Your father and I pay good money for you to go there instead of a normal public school you better be down here in five minutes or I am going to come up there," the loud female voice pierced his ears.

"Mom, I'm up. Jesus, I'm up!" Jensen shouts. He lies tangled up in a spider web of sheets. Sighing heavily; he unwinds himself from the bedding and starts the search for clothes. Strewn across the floor is about a month's worth of dirty clothes, his walls are covered in alternative rock band posters and buxom blondes in small bikinis. His 'homework' desk is piled with papers, drawings and his backpack; which remains unopened and unmoved amongst the pile. Careful to not step on any dirty clothes, he picks up a black tee shirt giving it a good strong sniff.

This will do, he thinks. He tosses on a pair of jeans and bounds down the stairs into the living room.

"Stop running in my house Jensen!" The female's voice commands.

"Alright all ready, I'm awake and down here aren't I?" Jensen quips as he makes his way to the kitchen and lumps down at a glossy elegant dining table. He looks over behind the island and catches a female's eyes piercing his soul.

"What mom? I didn't do anything." He says, defensively.

"You are so frustrating sometimes. I swear if you weren't my son I would smack your father's attitude out of you." She said, wagging her finger at him.

"But, you aren't my mother. You're just the crazy lady that agreed to raise me, Moreen. I still like you, a little." Jensen quipped slyly.

"You are the only pain in the ass I willingly tolerate. Now make like a banana and peel your way out of my sight. Do not be late to class." Moreen chuckled. Jensen rolled his eyes, sighed and hastily left the house.

As he walks, the houses become older and more dilapidated. He passes once shiny signs now defaced with graffiti. Jensen's mind wanders as he makes his way towards the Apache Academy.

"Why do we have to go here? Why do I have to go here? Why can't I be like the other kids in my neighborhood? I don't want to be special, or the son of Ambrose, I just want to be Jensen." As he walks through the dying neighborhood, a blacked out sedan creeps by.

"I've never seen that car running around here."

He watches the sedan creep slowly down the street. Jensen doesn't think twice about the mysterious car as he finally makes it to the intersection across the street from Apache Academy. He hears a faint bell from across the street and runs for it.

Time trickles by slowly as Jensen sits through his classes. He sits in the far left corner of his last class, science; there are empty seats on either side of him. His eyes are affixed on his desk when two young girls walk in and sit next to him. Both have long black hair, soft olive skin and strikingly similar features. The only differences between the two were their exotic eyes. One had vibrant, soft violet eyes; the other had piercing red irises, intense and fiery. He looked up to the girl that has taken the seat to his left.

"Hey Olivia, how's it going?" he smiles, turning slightly in his chair to face her.

"Oh you know, another day, another chance to waste away inside this building." Olivia smirked.

"I know that feeling; this is the biggest waste of time." He responded.

"Ugh, you two, can you ever not complain we come to class? You act like life is so hard. We're way too young for that." The girl on the other side interrupted.

"Shut up Maria." Jensen and Olivia replied at the same time.

"I hate you two, I don't know why I hang out with you guys." Maria retorted.

"You have to, I'm your sister and if I remember correctly, you're the one that is dating Jensen. So, you kind of have to hang out with him too." Olivia smirks at her sister. Jensen pinches Maria's cheeks.

"She has two very good points. You should be nicer to me too; I do take you to dinner almost every night." Jensen winks at Maria. "Yeah, well if you weren't so sexy, you'd have nothing else to keep me interested with." Maria winks back, sticking her tongue out at him and turning back in her chair.

"Are you three going to join my class now?" The teacher inquired. His circular framed bifocals slide down his round face as he moves through the desks. He stands next to Maria's desk. "We're having a fascinating class about the newly discovered time travel technique discovered by Mr. Jensen's father. I would love for you to participate in this learning experience. I don't know, maybe you will learn and be able to apply the knowledge into flipping your hamburgers." The teacher spoke condescendingly.

"Yes Mr. Luther, I would love to learn about how time travel will be able to increase my ability to work at a dead end job." Jensen responded despondently.

"Good, so where was I? Oh yes, this new time travel technology or technique is called time warping. The benefits, according to the Department of Time Justice, are that we would no longer need to carry warp plates or any of the bulky equipment items in use. This new discovery will change the way the world works. Do you kids think this will benefit or hinder society? Can you see the positives or any negatives from this discovery?" Mr. Luther asked the students.

"Mr. Luther?" asks Olivia, raising her hand.

"Yes Olivia, you have a comment or question?" Mr. Luther responds.

"Shouldn't we be worried about the potential use? I mean, at least with the current methods we can keep track of where people go and what they are doing in specific time periods, but if we are able to get more people to time warp, how are we going to keep track of all that? There are plenty of bad people in the world that could use this discovery and severely disrupt the past or even the future. It's a dangerous discovery. While I think it's cool that we discovered it, I think it's something we should definitely not be teaching on a broad curriculum in a school environment. Not to offend Jensen and his family, but history isn't our playground." Olivia smiles as she concludes her argument. Jensen rolls his eyes in her direction.

"Mr. James, do you have a counter argument? Maybe, Maria? I know you two like to contrast Olivia's opinions." Mr. Luther stares directly at Jensen.

"Sir, with all due respect, I think that hell just froze over. I agree with Olivia. I'm excited by science and scientific discovery, but this is a dangerous discovery. I mean, if this falls into the wrong hands or someone with ill intent can use this time travel technique, how are we going to stop them? I remember hearing my dad talk about how dangerous time warps were if they don't heavily screen those that use them. That's why he created the Department of Time Justice. Without regulation, if we teach people to travel through time without warp plates, how would we defend ourselves, our history? We couldn't, it would be impossible." Jensen responds calmly. Before Mr. Luther responds, the bell rings to end the school day.

Jensen, Maria and Olivia walk out of class and begin to make the trek out of the school. As the three walk out, Jensen freezes when he notices the black sedan he had seen on his way to school.

"What's up Jensen?" Maria asks.

"I saw that car earlier today; it was creeping down my street. I've never seen one like it before, at least not in my neighborhood." As Jensen explained, a well-dressed man emerged from the car. His hair is slicked back, black with a tinge of gray on left side above his hair. He has some stubble on his face, wrinkles across his brow and small crow's feet. His skin looks slightly weathered, like a man who has spent too much time in the sun. His suit is fitted, black, crisp, freshly pressed. He adjusts a matte black silk tie, carefully standing beside the car.

"Jensen, I'm giving you a ride home." The figure shouts out to Jensen, who in a burst of recognition, walks over.

"Dad, what's with the car? I saw you creeping around earlier. When did you get this?" Jensen interrogates him.

"These are our new department cars, pretty slick right? I'm not sure whose you saw driving around earlier; I've been at work all morning. It was probably just one of our new guys testing out the GPS." His father replied dismissively. "Let's get out of here; I think your mom said she would have us some early dinner ready." Ambrose gets into the car as Jensen slides into the front passenger seat. He glances around at the plush tan leather interior; the tinted windows blocking the outside worlds. The seat bolsters fit tightly around his body; the belt holds him in firmly as Ambrose accelerates rapidly out of the parking lot and towards the James' residence.

The trip that took Jensen the better part of half an hour on foot, takes only minutes in the black sedan. Ambrose slows to a crawl as the sedan eases into the driveway.

"You go on ahead Jensen; I have to make a phone call before I head in. You know your mother won't let me make a work related phone call once I go inside," Ambrose smiles at his son, grasping his phone. Jensen nods as he slides out of the black sedan. He saunters up the driveway, pulling out his key to unlock the door.

"Unlocked?" He thinks. *"I thought I locked it when I left, mom's going to be so mad if she finds out."* Jensen continues through the door, tossing his shoes to the side.

"Mom, Dad and I are home, he said you promised us an early dinner." Jensen shouts through the house. No response.

"Mom, where are you?"

"I bet she's napping or locked in the bath again." Jensen tells himself as he rushes up the stairs, skipping a step with each lunge upward. Jensen searches, but no sign of his mother anywhere.

"What in the world is going on?" He thinks, scratching his head at the bottom of the stairs. *"I better go get Dad, maybe Mom told him she was going to be somewhere and he forgot."* Jensen heads outside to talk to Ambrose but the black sedan is nowhere to be seen.

"What the hell is going on here?" He looks for around for a moment, and then heads back inside the house to look for his mother, Out of the corner

of his eye, he notices that the back sliding glass door is ajar.

"*I bet she's in the garden.*" Jensen quickly makes for the backyard. He steps out on the red brick patio. He looks towards the flower garden, no sign of his mother. He glances past the grass lawn and barbecue pit. Still, there is no sign of his mother anywhere around the house or yard. Then he looks towards the lone oak tree.

Jensen starts to dry heave over the side of the patio. He hunches over, stomach knotted in pain, as tears flow freely. He screams soundlessly, crippled by what he sees. Chained and nailed to the trunk of the tree is his mother in a thin, form fitting white dress which Jensen recognizes from the photos of his parents wedding day. Blood stains seep through the fabric; her arms are broken and tied backwards around the sides of the trunk. Her head is strapped with a chain, holding it looking forward out across the yard. A thick, crusty line of blood runs across her neck. Tears obscure his vision as he tries to swallow the growing lump in his throat. He slowly stands to take in the grisly scene. He notices a folded piece of paper, with a bow tied neatly to it flaps swaying in the breeze. Taking a deep breath, he walks to his mother's body and removes the piece of paper, slowly removing it.

History is no mystery; it is no place for you to tread. Continue with your research and your family will be dead. This is your warning Ambrose, stop your plans and bring your research to a close. The lives of millions outweigh the life and wealth of one. We won't stop until you do. – The Awakened

Jensen lets the paper fall as he turns back to the house. With his stomach in knots and drying tears, he shuts the glass sliding door behind him. *Where is Ambrose? Where did my Dad go?* Jensen collapses on the living room couch as his mind races with questions; the pain in his heart intensifies as the questions build.

Chapter 6

Jensen stood next to his mother's lifeless body to examine his work. Since he had discovered her, he had carefully cleaned off the blood from her soft, pale blue skin. He tried to clean the blood off of her dress, leaving it slightly stained. The blood soaked chains and straps were now heaped in a massive pile at the trunk.

Jensen carefully bent down to one knee and kissed her forehead

"I love you Mom. I'll find the person who did this." He promised as if trying to reassure her that he would not let her death be in vain. He carefully grasped one edge of the sheet and draped it over his mother's body, gently tucking it underneath her, repeating with the other corner. He took one last look at her face.

Still serene and beautiful, even in death, he thought, as he took the last bit to fold over her face. Her body is now closed off from the elements and the world. He slowly stands and walks back into the house.

"Nothing seems out of place," he thinks, as he wanders around looking for any signs of foul play. He can't shake the thoughts of wondering where his father had gone to so fast. *"Perhaps, his work call required him to run back to the office. That wouldn't be the first time. I should've sat in the car and waited for him. Still, why didn't he come home last night?"*

A loud slam from outside the house startles Jensen, who rushes to the window to peer through the blind at the black sedan in the driveway. As Jensen watches he sees his father wait as another sedan pulls into the driveway. His father greets four men exiting the other black sedan.

"Who are these men? I've never seen or heard my dad mention anyone else he works with". He wonders carefully peering through the blinds. Jensen watches as all five men turn to enter the house. He slides away from the blinds and makes his way quietly up to his room.

Ambrose leads the four men through the house and into the backyard. He freezes when he spots the empty tree. The four men behind him all stop, exchanging looks.

"It looks like my son knows. We need to make sure he doesn't know anything about who did this." Ambrose engages each of the men in an icy stare. They nod silently in agreement. The four men separate and follow as Ambrose purposefully walks through back into the house. All five men stop at the base of the stairs; Ambrose addresses them.

"Wait here. I'm going to run upstairs and see if he's still home. If he is, I'll talk to him and see if he knows what happened. We'll decide what to do next depending on his answer." The men silently nod in agreement. Ambrose nervously heads up the stairs.

"I wish I could go back and change all this, but it's too late now. I'm getting everything I've ever desired. She knew. She always knew, no matter what the cost, I'd sacrifice for my personal success". His thoughts cloud his head as he knocks softly on his son's door.

"Yeah, I'm in here." Jensen shouted. His father walks into the room and the two stand facing each other, only a few feet apart.

"Did you see her body?" Jensen resentfully asked

"I saw it the other morning when I went home from work. I had to leave. The sight was too much to bear. I had to get the authorities involved. I know it wasn't the right way to handle things to have you come home, but I'm still in disbelief." Ambrose explained.

"How much do you know about them, about the Awakened? Who are those men downstairs?" Jensen knows that any response he gets from Ambrose will be a lie, as it always has been. All his life, Ambrose has lied to him. Now with his mother dead, he prepared himself for another string of lies.

"I need to be careful. I don't know what this man is capable of," thought Jensen.

"Those men down there, Jensen, those are some of my esteemed research colleagues. We've developed into great friends through our latest discovery. As far as the Awakened, they are just a new maniacal terrorist group. They are trying to bully us into not using our latest discovery in time travel. They feel we aren't the right group of people to wield such power. We are though; we can control the world with this!" Ambrose's excitement is palpable. Jensen takes a hesitant step away from his father, surprised as heard his father mention anything of power with his discoveries.

"All those rumors," Jensen thought. *"All those rumors, through all those years, they're all true. My*

father is a maniac. No, no, there is no way he could be like that. My mom never would have stood for it. Oh my god, mom." He swallows, clenching his fists.

"Son, Jensen, my son, there is nothing to be afraid of here. We will have money beyond all belief; there will be nobody to stop us. It's unfortunate your mother fell in with the wrong crowd. I offered her every opportunity Jensen; she's just going to be an innocent casualty in all this when it's over. If I could have been here to stop it; I would have."

Ambrose reaches towards him, letting his hand rest on his shoulder, to reassure him that he could be trusted, but Jensen removes it disdainfully

"I don't know who the fuck you are or what the fuck you're up to. My mother once loved a man who was trying to better the world and save people's lives with his research, but you, what you're saying to me. Who the hell are you? What are you trying to do? Why is my Mom dead?" Jensen's voice fills with rage as the question pour from his mouth.

"This can't be happening to me. Who would believe me? What should I do? I'm outnumbered. I'm not a good fighter. I need to run." Panic seethed through his body.

"Jensen, come downstairs with me. I'll introduce you to my team and we can bring you down to the Time Department and you can see firsthand the discoveries we're making. We're going to change the world son, and the best part is, we'll be in control of the world." Ambrose spoke,

63

trying to reassure his son again, but Jensen quickly sidesteps, never taking his eyes off of his father.

"Don't you fucking touch me; you killed your wife didn't you? You killed my own mother, didn't you? Who the hell are you? What the fuck do you want with me?" Jensen sensed his father's wrongdoing.

"Jensen, calm down Come downstairs with me and meet my guys. They'll reassure you and then we can all sit down and talk about what's going on." Ambrose moved and Jensen deflected.

"Alright, you go down first, let me calm down for a minute." Jensen calmly responded, masking his agitation.

"Fine, be downstairs in two minutes or I'm going to bring you down there," Ambrose sighed as he slowly crept away.

"For fuck's sake give me a couple minutes to calm down Dad!" Jensen shouted at his father.

He knew what he was about to do would send his life into a blur of epic proportion.

"I just have to get to the library so I can figure out what he discovered. I can't let this go on. I need to figure out how Ambrose was so easily able to kill the woman that I thought he loved." Breathing deeply, Jensen carefully places his hands on the top of the window, using his thumb and index figure to unlock it. He spares one last look at his bedroom door, listening for sounds of Ambrose.

This is the perfect time to do this. Jensen thinks. He quietly slides it open and swings one leg out and looks down. He has a clear path off the roof and down to the grass.

"I hope I don't get hurt. Otherwise this is a failed plan from the start. Just remember to roll forward." Hearing footsteps, he decides there is no time like the present.

Jensen slides through the window onto the roof and takes three quick giant paces to the right and without a second thought, rushes off the side of the house. Jensen tucks his knees and propels himself forward as he makes contact with the ground. He rolls over in a somersault once before quickly bounding to his feet. He doesn't even stop to look back as he races up and across the street.

"Shit!" Ambrose shouts back throughout Jensen's empty bedroom. "Get your stuff ready gentlemen, he's running!"

Ambrose flies out of his son's room and down the stairs, passing the four men who quickly follow him out of the door. "I know exactly where he is going. We're going to let him meet up with his little friends for a few minutes so he thinks he got away. Then we'll get rid of all of them. No loose ends." Ambrose exclaimed.

"I'm going to make a phone call on our way there. He's going to Olivia and Maria's. You guys know the Jima's; it looks like the ones trying to stop me are going to be the first ones to get a visit from me." Ambrose and the men leave in the five sedans singe file, Ambrose leading in a creeping pace.

"I really want to give them all time to try to plan something. It will make arresting them for conspiracy so much easier. It will also allow me to pin the murder of Moreen on Annalise. She will finally rue the day she double crossed me."

Ambrose's mind races with excitement and anger. He fumbles with around with his phone, scrolling quickly, as his screen *clicks* stopping on the name Edmund Jima highlighted in blue. A wry smile spreads across his face.

Jensen breathes heavily as he comes to a stop in a small field. He drops to one knee, resting his hand on the ground; the tall grass camouflaging him. He looks up slowly as he hears cars approaching. He carefully parts the grass as the string of cars roll by.

"I've eluded them for now." he thinks. Jensen waits for a moment before standing up and continuing on his path. *"I've got to make it to the Jima's. They're the only ones that can help me figure this out."*

Chapter 7

Olivia Jima lay on her bed with her extremely loud and over oversized headphones on her ears, wearing her Ramones t-shirt, cuffed blue jeans, which showed off her butterfly tattoos on both ankles, neatly above the top of her red low top canvas sneakers. Olivia chuckles slightly at Maria who is waving her arms angrily at her. Huffing Maria turns and slams the door loudly. "Don't slam the door bitch!" Olivia shouts at the closed door.

"Mom, Olivia used my make-up again. I tried to talk to her but she just blew me off with her loud music. I'm so sick of this." Maria whined at her mother.

"Just relax Maria. I will go talk to her again in a little while. She is probably just in one of those moods she gets in. You know it always has to be her against the world or something foolish." Anna Jima, the elegant, beautiful matriarch calmly told Maria.

"Whatever mom, hopefully she listens to you this time." Maria stormed out, leaving Anna standing in the luxurious open kitchen pondering how best to deal with yet another feud between her teenage daughters.

"Hello, my lovely," Edmund Jima strolls into the kitchen, wrapping his arms around Anna's waist. His slicked back hair reflects the light from the kitchen He presses his lips against Anna's cheek, his pencil thin mustache, just as black and slick as his hair touches her cheek lightly.

"I'm going to shave that horrendous thing off your face when you're asleep." Anna leans away, running her finger down across his mustache and presses it on his lips.

"No, no, my dear, I've really grown quite fond of it. You look stressed Anna, what's the matter?" Edmund pulls his wife gently to his side.

"Our daughters are going to drive me to alcoholism or drug smuggling. Maybe both if I'm lucky." She wraps her arms around his neck. He returns the embrace.

"So I guess Olivia is being rebellious again? I'll go talk to her; maybe she will listen to me this time. It has to be all that noise she listens to." Edmund smiles as he kisses Anna. He releases from their hug and makes his way upstairs.

Olivia lies on her bed, mouthing the lyrics to a song blaring through her headphones. She's vigorously mashing the buttons of her cellphone, texting someone on the other end. Her music is drowning out the sound of Edmund bashing his fist against the door while jiggling the locked handle. Olivia's phone vibrates in her hand, catching her attention.

TEXT FROM MARIA:

Hey dumb ho, Dad's been knocking at your door for like five minutes. You are so fucking dead when you open the door.

"Shit," Olivia silently mouths as she tosses her headphones onto her pillow to unlock the door. Olivia pulls it open to see her father leaning against the door frame.

"Olivia, how many times do I have to tell you that we don't lock our doors in this household? We don't use each other's things. If you want make-up to use or if you run out, what are you supposed to do?" Edmund asks impatiently.

"Dad, I wasn't out I just wanted to try that shade of lipstick. I'm not going to go buy something if I may not like how it looks. That's wasteful." Edmund maneuvers his way past his daughter into her room.

"What's wasteful, Olivia, is what you're doing with your life. You should be doing your schoolwork like your sister. You'll never get into college with your work ethic." Edmund says, rummaging through her notebooks and papers that are strewn about her desk.

"Dad, we have this discussion every time Maria complains to you and Mom about something I'm doing or something she thinks I've done. It's getting old." Olivia's frustration leaks through her voice.

"Watch your tone with me young lady. Give me your music. You can have it back in a week." Edmund motions with extended arms.

"Dad…seriously?" Olivia questions. Her father stays in the same position and Olivia rolls her eyes tossing her music player and headphones into his hand.

"Ok, and now you're grounded." Edmund storms past her and out of her room. Olivia shakes with anger, tossing herself onto her bed. Her phone vibrates.

TEXT FROM JENSEN:

Hey, are you guy's home? I need a place to stay, something fucking crazy is going on!!

Olivia reads the text, her fingers quickly begin to mash out her response:

Yeah, we're all home, the dictators and your whore girlfriend. What's up?

Olivia checks her phone, sets it on her stomach, and then checks it again. A few minutes go by before she gets a response.

TEXT FROM JENSEN:

My Mom is dead.

"Holy shit!" Olivia blurted, running out of her room and down the stairs where her family is watching television. She tosses her phone at her dad.

"Dad, read that!" Taking note of his daughter, he reads it and then slides the phone over to Anna. They look at one another, perplexed.

"Tell him he has a place to stay over here. He doesn't need to be consoled via emotionless texts if he's being serious." The calm demeanor of her parents troubles Olivia, but she sensed that she might be overreacting over the text. Olivia ran back upstairs punching the dial key on her phone next to Jensen's name. The phone rings for an eternity before clicking over to his voicemail, but she doesn't leave a message.

Edmund and Anna leave for the kitchen, leaving an oblivious Maria behind, blaring music out of Olivia's headphones. She scrolls through her phone and selects Jensen from her contact list. She slides the phone up between the earpiece and her ear. The phone rings, and rings before going to voicemail.

"Hey, it's just me, wanting to know what's up for today. Call me back. Kisses." Once off, she looks around to see she is alone in the living room. She shrugs her shoulders once, and zones out to the show.

In the kitchen, Edmund and Anna discuss what to do if, in fact, Jensen's text is real and what course of action to take if it turns out to be a dramatic teenager running away from home.

"If it's not a false alarm, we're going to have to tell him what we know about Ambrose." Edmund nods.

"You mean we're going to have to convince him that we know suspicious things about his father. We can't lead on that we know more, much more than we can ever let him know. It will be damaging to our cause with The Awakened." Anna responds. They discuss a plan for their They discuss how to explain to Jensen about the details of his mother's death and not waiting for Jensen to discuss how he found her or his interaction with his father afterwards.

"I think we just have to convince him that we are on his side, which if he is struggling emotionally with this loss, won't be too hard to do." Anna pauses, as if something is on her mind.

"I'm going to go tell Olivia to be patient and calm when Jensen gets here. We know she's the one that will care more." Anna starts to leave the kitchen.

"Just, don't tell her Anna. She's a loose cannon with information." Edmund sternly suggests.

"Relax, if anything, you know that I am more than capable of handling this with everything we've just gone through." She smiles slyly as she leaves.

Edmund whips out his cellphone and quickly dials a number.

"I've told you to not call me directly unless there's an emergency." A mysterious voice answered.

"I know, but we have a problem. The young man, he's on his way. He found his mother, not Ambrose. How do we play this?" Edmunds asked quietly.

"Well don't tell him anything Edmund. Christ, you know what you have to do. Let it play out. Ambrose will come for him. Convince Jensen you're on his side. This is your ass if you fuck this up. I'm not in the business of covering up messes." The voice cuts off with an audible click. Edmund goes into the living room and plops next to his impervious daughter on the couch. At least he has one daughter he doesn't have to worry about.

Anna walks into Olivia's room, where caught off guard; she quickly tosses a journal underneath her pillow.

"Olivia, if you're writing in your journal about Jensen again, we will talk about that later. We need to talk about how to act when he gets here, you know, in case he is telling the truth." She sits next to Olivia. "Jensen could be going through a range of emotions right now if his mother is dead. We tried to get a hold of Ambrose but as usual, his father

72

didn't answer. Jensen is going to be in a very fragile emotional state. I need you to understand this because he may not be the happy go lucky, friendly kid you're used to." Olivia rolls her eyes.

"Mom, stop. I'm not Maria. I'm not an idiot. I understand all that. Jensen is my friend, I hope this isn't real, but it seems to be legit, he isn't even answering his phone." She scoots next to her mom and pats her on the knee.

"Ok, your father just felt that I should remind you. I know you mean well." Anna awkwardly puts her arm around Olivia, then quickly releases it and moves to the door.

"Oh, and stop daydreaming about your sister's boyfriend. If he was interested in you, he would be your boyfriend and not your best friend. You can do better." Anna tosses out these words as Olivia stares at her in disbelief. Olivia unearths her journal from under a pillow, opens up a page and reviews some previously written down words:

Day Whatever,

Parents are still weird. Sister is a bitch.

Day Whatever and a half,

Parents are acting really strange. If Hitler was alive, he would work for my parents. My sister is still dating Jensen and she still treats him like a worthless being. I should break them up. We have more fun when we hang out than they do. What does he even see in her? Oh Jensen, it could be worse, you could have a smart and pretty girlfriend and not one with big tits. Maybe you're just a simple boy.

Olivia sighs, tossing her journal back to the side. Her phone vibrates.

TEXT FROM JENSEN:

I'm outside about to ring the doorbell.

Olivia catapults off her bed as the doorbell rings.

Chapter 8

"Ok Jensen. One more time. Ambrose, your own father, killed your mother, and he's framing one of the political groups that oppose his use and discovery of time warping? This doesn't sound remotely like your father." Edmund repeated clearly. Anna, Maria and Olivia huddled on the couch around the distraught young man.

"Look, I've told you this a few times already. He was with four men that I had never seen before; they were all driving the blacked out sedans. My father said he saw my mother but then left the house the day prior. Nothing lines up Mr. Jima; he has to be hiding something. He wanted to talk to me about these 'Awakened' with the men downstairs but it didn't feel right. I came here because I know you have been friends with my parents for years. You have to know something about what is happening." Jensen was distraught.

Ding! Maria removes her phone from her pocket and begins sliding her finger across the screen. Edmund looks at her disapprovingly.

"Relax Edmund; it's just a friend from school asking about our class assignment." Maria rolls her eyes. "I think I believe him Dad. I've never known Jensen to make up wild accusations. Who would be able to make up those details about how they found their own mother dead?"

Edmund rubs his hands on his face. "Girls, Anna, I think I need to speak to Jensen alone. We have some very serious things to discuss. Please close the door on your way out." Anna stands to chauffer the girls out.

"Yes dear. Come on girls; let's go order a pizza or something for a late dinner. I think it's going to be a long night." As she walks out with her arms around the girls she looks back and nods at her husband before shutting the doors.

"Jensen, I need you to promise me that what I'm about to tell you never leaves this room. You must commit this to memory. My girls cannot know what I'm about to tell you. I need you to promise, to swear on your life that if you repeat any of this conversation we're about to have, you will go to your grave for it. I was hoping it wouldn't come to this but I need your trust now, do I have your promise, your trust?" Edmund slides onto the sofa next to Jensen; and looks him dead in the eyes.

"I will do whatever it takes to avenge my mother." Jensen replies with hate-filled anger. Edmund pats Jensen on the knee before pacing around the room.

"The Awakened, we didn't kill your mother. We've been compiling evidence against your father for quite some time. We don't know who is behind his research in the Department of Time Justice, but someone got to your father. For the past decade or so, he has received a lot of funding for discovering new ways to travel through time. We've recently found out that this new time warp method is going to be used to alter the past of Apache. We don't know what the endgame is, but we believe they are going to use time warping to not only have power over Apache but to eventually alter history to the point where people like Anna and me, and now you, never existed to oppose their mission." Edmund paused looking at Jensen, whose jaw was slightly hanging, open. "I personally have done everything I can to keep my girls and you from becoming entrenched in this situation, but it's obvious that you are destined to be involved. So I'm going to let you in on the secret to time warping. You are going to be hunted Jensen. Your father will not stop until anyone that has knowledge of his research in the Department is exterminated. Once I give you this information you must use it. You must get to somewhere safe. From there it is up to you to stand and fight against your father. This is a lot to ask of someone your age Jensen, you have to understand that should you accept your destiny, you will be in incredible danger." Edmund stopped pacing and looked at Jensen who stood slowly wiping his hands on the front of his pants leg.

"You have my word Mr. Jima. I will honor my destiny for my mother." Jensen spoke, shaking hands.

"Let's go get some food. Anna and I have a lot to tell you and we better do it quickly. Ambrose will already know you're here. He's been after us for at least a year now. Ever since one of our scientists defected to the Department's cause." Edmund and Jensen exit to rejoin the family.

Maria sit as the table, smiling occasionally and fiddling with her phone, shooting the occasional glances at her parents and her sister and Jensen who have laid waste to the pizza and breadsticks.

"Come on everyone," Anna speaks to her girls and Jensen. "We have some things to show you." As the rest of the family and Jensen go into the living room, Maria slides her fingers across her phone one more time, making sure that everyone is outside of the kitchen before taking a picture of her beaming smile with her phone. After gently clicking the top lock button, she saunters into the living room, casually sitting down in a recliner, as her parents sit on the sofa and Jensen and Olivia plop down onto the hardwood floor. Maria casually snaps another photo, this time of her family and Jensen sitting on the living room. Edmund looks at Maria.

"I need you to pay attention Maria; this affects you more than you already know. Jensen, what we're about to show you is the latest discovery by your father. With it you can travel to any point in time, any point in history, and you have the potential to change the future. This is Ambrose's ultimate goal. We still don't know if he has been influenced by anyone, or if this is a power move of his own accord." Edmund looks at Anna, who smiles and begins to speak.

"We formed The Awakened over ten years ago when the Department of Time Justice was announced and they proclaimed their mission involving newly discovered time travel technology. Ever since then they have been veiled in a huge secrecy on their mission. They've started to become influential in the day to day crime fighting operations and are starting to train our own police forces. There is something greater going on, we have evidence to prove that, but we don't know what it is for certain. It definitely now includes Ambrose's latest time warp discovery. We know how to do it, but our fight lies here on the political front. We want you three to learn this technique and join in the struggle. We know this a lot to ask of you, but after recent events, we can't see any other way around it." Anna stands up, taking a deep breath. Maria glances up from her phone, her violet eyes sparkling in the screen's glow.

Edmund removes a folded piece of paper and a small plastic bag containing five black pills and hands it over to Jensen to read.

To those who wish to change the future:

Located in this plastic bag are five pills. These pills are from a classified origin. Their effects on the body allow an ordinary human to alter their minds to see temporal rifts in the space-time continuum. Once an individual is able to see these rifts, the pills allow a person's DNA to pass through the rift unaltered. Whatever place in time the individual is focusing on in their mind, they will be transported through by entering through these rifts. The side effects are unknown as they have only been tested in a limited capacity. Take these pills and use them in your fight. My position in the Department has been compromised. My time is short. I hope these pills find their uses to keep Apache and the future of all people in the world safe.

Jensen hands the paper to Olivia, whose red eyes scan the paper quickly, nods as she finishes skimming the letter. Maria slowly moves to Olivia's side and snatches the letter, reading it just as quickly as her sister. Edmund holds out the pills to the three of them.

"This is your destiny. You three are our only hope in this world. Anna and I have to stay here and fight. I know we don't know of any dangers associated with these pills, with this discovery, but we fear time is of the essence. Please take one now, we will figure the rest out as it goes along." The three teens swallow the pills in unison as they all look at each other, nervous with anticipation. The silence is broken by Edward's cellphone who stares at the lit up screen reading Ambrose.

"Hello Ambrose," Edmund answers softly.

"Hello old friend. I believe my son is over at your house right now." Ambrose replied confidently.

"I don't think so old friend. I haven't seen him in a few weeks. Is there something I can do for you?" Edmund motions to Anna to get the three teens moving.

"No my friend, he's there. I think you should walk him out your front door now." Ambrose calmly explained.

"I can't do that Ambrose." A soft click goes off in Edmund's ear. "Hello? Hello? Ambrose?" Edmund quickly rises; turning to run around the sofa as the front door to the house explodes with a fury. The door shatters as thousands of wood splinters fly through the hallway, sending Edmund flying to the floor, covering him in shards of wood.

"Anna RUN!" Edmund shouts agonizingly. He sees four men rush in through the entryway with Ambrose walking in slowly behind them.

"Why, hello Edmund. So charming to see you here; where is my son?" Ambrose strolls into the house, casually addressing the wounded Edmund.

Anna is frantically looking through the dresser in her bedroom with the three teens who were nervously watching the bedroom door.

"Jensen, here, take this." Anna tosses Jensen a gloss black revolver with an ivory white handle, who catches it easily, examining it.

"I don't know when your pills will take effect, but you three most go. I have to go with Edmund now. We will always be there for you." Jensen started to reach towards Anna but she runs out the door to help her husband.

Jensen turns to the sisters.

"I think we need to go." Jensen rushes to the bedroom window and pushes it open, quickly climbing out as Olivia follows. Maria, behind them, pulls the window shut. Olivia turns and looks up locking eyes with her sister. Maria takes out her phone taking a picture of the two of them. She looks at her phone before smiling at Olivia. Jensen and Olivia exchange bewildered looks. They watch as Maria walks out the bedroom door. Olivia opens her mouth to speak, but Jensen interrupts.

"We have to get out of here Olivia; we can figure the rest out later." Jensen grabs Olivia's hand and they jump off the roof.

Inside the house Anna slowly walks down the stairs, meeting Ambrose's eyes.

"Hello my dear Anna." Ambrose smiles up at Anna.

"I don't think I've ever been your dear anything, Ambrose." She replied, sliding the ivory revolver off her hip and squeezing the trigger. Suddenly, Anna's revolver falls out of her hand and bounces down the stairs with a thud to the floor in front of Ambrose. Anna, shaking, raises her hand in front of her, seeing Ambrose smirking through the smoking hole of flesh in her hand. She glances behind her to see Maria's purple eyes staring her down over the barrel of a smooth Beretta handgun at the top of the stairs.

"Maria!" Anna cries painfully.

"Walk down the stairs carefully or I'll spill your pitiful brains." Maria retorts, hate and anger coloring her voice.

"Ah, there's my girl. How are you my dear? I loved the pictures you've sent me." Ambrose smiles conspiratorially.

"Ambrose; are you going to keep your promise to me?" Maria picks her way down the stairs, keeping the gun barrel trained at the mother and stops in front of Ambrose who gently kisses her on her forehead.

"I made a promise, didn't I my little flower. You've delivered most of what I wanted and now I will give you anything you've ever wanted." Ambrose returns his gaze to Anna who ran to Edmund, still huddled on the floor, now flanked by the four men.

"Take them to the prison; I'll have the Department draw up the conspiracy papers." Ambrose directs his cronies. They grab the parents violently and rush them out the entryway.

As they leave the house, watching the men force Edmund and Anna inside the black sedans Marie shows Ambrose the picture of Olivia and Jensen escaping.

"Anything you've ever wanted." Ambrose purrs into Maria's ear.

Jensen and Olivia, hiding behind the bushes of a neighboring house, notice the sparkling fury of Maria's eyes in the porch light.

"We're in this together." Jensen quietly breathes towards Olivia as a small wave of dust forms behind them.

"Let's do this." Olivia stutters, wiping tears from her face as they grab each other's hand and crawl through the wave of dust. Everything around them blurs together.

Chapter 9

"Maria." Jensen's eyes open with a flash. He can picture her clearly, standing at the window, while he and Olivia escaped long ago. He eyeballed the apartment, wondering how Maria had convinced him that she was Olivia.

"Why didn't I notice the difference in the eyes, why was I so easily tricked?" Jensen sits up in the bed slowly. *"I wonder if she is still here."* A small beam of light snuck in through the crack in the door, lying on the comforter. He sighed and swung his legs over the bed, looking for clothes to wear.

"Jensen, my love; are you awake yet?" Maria's voice softly carries through the apartment. Jensen pauses, his mind filling with thoughts of escape, confrontation, and some way out of this mess.

"Yes, my dear. I'm going to grab a shower quick. What are we having for breakfast?" A single bright light comes on in his closet as he opens the sliding doors. To his left, row of black jeans neatly folded over their hangars lines the bottom closet rod. Folded above lies a row of white collared shirts, neatly pressed and hung neatly, perfectly spaced out. He grabs pants and a shirt, then turns to his right and grabs a black bowtie and belt off a small table. He reaches up and grabs a black Stetson hat. A gloss black revolver with ivory handles slides off the shelf. Jensen reacts quickly, catching the revolver in his hand. He carefully examines it as it rests in his hand.

Jensen's mind drifts back to years ago, back to when he was a young teen, and hiding in a bedroom. A mother's eyes locked onto him as the same revolver flew through the air towards him. He remembers Maria and Olivia standing by his side. Worst of all, he can see Maria's smile as she shut the window and walked out of the bedroom. He can see her violet eyes looking out as he and Olivia snuck out through their first time warp.

"Things are going to get a bit interesting now." Jensen wraps the revolver up in his pants and shirt as he grabs a long black trench coat from a hook and proceeds out the bedroom door. Jensen slides into the bathroom, carefully shutting the door behind him.

"Yes, that's three breakfast rolls, an order of bacon, and a gallon of orange juice, we're hungry, so make it snappy," Maria chuckled forcefully. In the kitchen, she hangs up the phone as she gazes at the bathroom door, water echoing lightly from it. She unfolds a black towel, revealing three large knives, a small vial of unknown liquid, and a syringe. She caresses the blades of the knives, occasionally looking back through the kitchen towards the bathroom door.

"It's finally going to be over. I'm putting an end to this. No more Edmund, no more Anna, no Olivia, and finally no more Jensen James ruining my future. I'll finally get to be Mrs. Ambrose James. We'll have a fairy tale wedding and life, oh how this has been long overdue." She smiles brightly, tucking her chin into her shoulder. As she continues to caress the knives, she quickly snaps back to reality. Ambrose promised her the perfect life, endless money, endless power, and anything you

could ever want. Maria brings the vial up into the light and squints at the small writing.

Caution: Radioactive, may cause cancer, heavy gamma radiation. Contains; Americium-243, handle with extreme caution.

With her free hand, she slides the plastic cover off the needle tip of the syringe and plunges the needle into the top, pulling gently on the top. Gradually, a thick silvery-white liquid fills the syringe. Maria pauses as the water stops in the bathroom and discards the vial into the sink. She carefully places the syringe back on to the black towel and picks up each knife carefully examining the blades, placing each one in a sheath along her waist. She pats each sheath carefully before sliding her leather jacket back over her arms, leaving it unbuttoned.

Reaching quickly, Maria grasps one of the knives and slashes the air. She slides the knife back in the sheath and turns her attention back to the black towel and syringe. Maria wraps the syringe gently, lightly grasping the towel. A larger, tougher hand slides over hers, covering them completely. Maria gulps as she turns to see Jensen, his black Stetson hat casting a shadow over his stone gray eyes that now peered into Maria's.

"Jensen," she whispered.

"Hello Maria." Jensen replied, angrily.

Maria's eyes widen and her hands tremble as she takes a step back to stand directly in front of Jensen. Both of them are still holding onto the towel wrapped syringe, staring each other down.

"How did you know it was me?" Maria asked, breaking the silence. Jensen snarled at her.

"Your eyes, I'll never forget those eyes. The way they twinkled that night, so many years ago, as Olivia and I escaped through our first rift. Seeing you stand there, next to my father, Ambrose. The same day I found out he killed my mother. How could you?" Jensen stepped towards her, gripping the towel tighter. Maria removed one of her hands to grasp the hiding knife, using the other hand to grip the towel tighter.

"Silly Jensen, you've never understood. You never wanted to have the perfect life. You were always so prideful, had to do everything yourself. Earn everything yourself. That's not me. All I've ever had to do throughout the years was to get rid of you. Every single time, you always escaped Hector; you've always been one step ahead of me. Not today, not anymore. I'm going to get what I deserve!" Maria shrieked, lunging towards him with a knife.

Jensen takes a quick step to the left grabbing the towel into his hand as Maria's hand holding one of the steel blade knives narrowly misses catching Jensen. She spins rapidly, unsheathing another knife, slashing wildly as Jensen backpedals. He tosses the black towel into the air, grabbing Maria's arms, knocking one of her knives to the floor. The two struggle briefly as the towel begins its descent. Maria frees her arms and places a solid side-kick to Jensen's ribs, sending him flying through the kitchen. She snatches the towel out of the air, flipping the syringe into her hand. Maria leaps towards Jensen, raising her hand above her head aiming the syringe at his heart. Her arm strikes downward as he raises his, their wrists meeting in the middle. Jensen grabs Maria by the throat, and tosses her into the hallway.

Maria lunges back towards Jensen, trying to catch him with her knife in one hand and the Americium syringe in the other He dodges her advances again, his reactions becoming quicker with each movement. He catches her wildly swinging arms and kicks her firmly in the chest, throwing her back into the wall with a sickening thud, crumpling to the floor.

"Get up bitch!" He shouts as Maria, cackling, uses the wall to pull herself up. She drops the knife, her hand holding the loaded syringe. She smiles as she wipes her mouth on her sleeve.

"One more night with you would have been nice. It would have been like when we were in high school all over again. However, after I kill you, I'm going to cut it off as a memoir." Maria charges him, chopping her arm downward slashing wildly. Reflexively, he blocks each swing of the syringe as Maria backs him through the kitchen with a jumping roundhouse kicks. The kick echoes as Maria connects with Jensen's arm. Maria pursues Jensen as he continues to back away from her advances. Their shadows dance feverishly, casting a martial arts ballet on the walls of the apartment. Maria spins around unsheathing her last knife off her belt, slashing the air between them. Jensen grabs Maria's left arm with his right hand and proceeds to grab her right arm with his left hand, engaged in a life or death struggle. Jensen uses his weight and size to get Maria to push her arms down to her side, driving the syringe carefully into her hip. He then lunges forward, connecting with a firm head-butt to the upper portion of Maria's nose.

Maria moaned and dropped unconscious to the floor as blood streamed from her nose. Jensen bent down, checking her jugular.

"There's still a pulse." He mutters. Maria's body starts to convulse causing Jensen to take a step back. Looking down at her left hip, he sees the syringe firmly embedded into her leg. He watches as Maria's body succumb to the intense radiation of the Americium. Her body slowly ceases to convulse as her veins become visible through her skin. Her body tightens as a light smoke emanates from her mouth as the Americium slowly cooks Maria from the inside out.

Suspecting the Maria wasn't alone, he rushes through the apartment gathering supplies. He finds a small bottle of *Centella* and *Motrin*, in the bathroom. In the bedroom, he finds a black ammunition belt and a box of silver plated ammunition; he grabs similar set of clothes, and stumbles on a few stacks of money in the dresser, tossing everything in a duffle bag.

"This should last me for a while," he thinks. A belt buckle with a gold etching depicting an eagle soaring above a canyon catches his eye. Jensen removes the buckle from a belt, taking in the image before tossing it back on the bed. As he starts to leave the apartment, he stops briefly at Maria's charred remains.

"My perfect life is freedom for all people." He accesses the door panel. The large metal locks creak and thud, as Jensen looks back towards Maria's body one last time.

"For my mother,"

Chapter 10

Hector leaned carefully around the corner, staring at the outline of Jensen James in a Stetson hat and trench coat. Jensen turned briefly looking in Hector's direction before walking away. Hector motions cautiously to his team, who start to creep along in the shadows towards Jensen's apartment.

"Let's check on Maria first, and then follow him." Hector and the team stop in front of the door as Henry saunters over to a small panel to the right of the doors. Crouching on one knee, he removed a black keypad from his cargo pocket and carefully inserts two electrode cables into the keypad and then connects them onto the panel. Henry's fingers begin rapidly flying across the keypad, and then stop as he looks up expectantly. The large, locking beams slid open with loud thuds. Henry quickly unhooks the electrodes from the panel and walks back to join the others.

As Hector and twins entered the apartment, they were greeted by a sulfuric and charcoal odor. The twins gagged as Hector held his hand over his mouth and nose, noticing the burnt remains of Maria. He took a deep breath.

"There isn't anything for us to find here." Hector directs the twins back out of the apartment, where Henry is still standing.

"Close it Henry. We need to get after him now. I'm going to have to make a call to Ambrose while we track him." Henry gags as his stomach churns as the smell that wafts through the door. He quickly runs to the panel, connecting the electrodes from the keypad, making the door slam shut. Henry yanks the electrodes off the panel and walks quickly to catch up with Hector and the twins.

Hector, Henry and the twins return to following Jensen, along a walkway that leads to an atrium surrounded by large, glass skyscrapers. Henry stops to look up towards the massive opening hundreds of feet above them, slamming into Hector. Hector, frozen, his gaze affixed on a far off figure leaning against the trunk of a bent over willow tree. The twins have removed their sidearm and now have trained their pieces on their figure. Henry brings his head down, to see what has frozen his colleagues.

"Jensen James, I have a warrant for your arrest," yelled Hector as he removed his revolver from his hip. "We have you outnumbered and outgunned. I recommend you surrender."

Hector smiles slightly, exchanging glances with the twins. Hector and his men hold their firearms locked firmly on to Jensen.

"That's a rather tempting offer Hector. Surrender now to delay my inevitable death at the hands of my own father, or take my chances engaging you for the first time in the decades you've chased me. I know you what you ultimately want Hector, so I'm going to have to politely refuse your recommendation." Jensen pushes himself off the tree, digging in his coat pocket and removing a small, tightly wrapped cigar, and a stainless steel lighter etched with a golden eagle. Flipping the top open, a generous flame engulfs the tip of the cigar. Flipping the lid shut, the tosses it carelessly on the ground. As the cigar embers burn brightly as Jensen takes another hit, his hand slides down to his ivory handles of his revolver. The men lock eyes.

The Luna gang patiently waits for Jensen to make the first move who lightly puffs on the brown cigar. Hector takes a deep breath and scans down the sight of his revolver. The wood grain handle grasped firmly in his right hand, the stainless silver barrel gently reflects the sunlight. Both James and Jeff hold Beretta 9mm handguns, their massive frames creating a large target area. Hector slowly shifts his stance, minimizing his profile towards Jensen. Henry stands a few feet behind the rest of the team, his eyes sweeping the atrium.

I need to hide. I should have brought my gun. Henry worries, as he slides away from the confrontation. *Maybe I can get back to the van, get my gun and make it back before anything happens.* Henry turns and sprints away, his boots smack the ground heavily as he exits the atrium. Neither Hector nor the twins make a move, as their eyes and sidearms still lock onto Jensen.

"I'm going to give you another chance Jensen. I can guarantee you safe passage to the prison until your father comes and gets you. He wants you to answer for your crimes. He knows you killed Moreen. That's why he's after you, no other reason. You'll probably just get life in prison, but that's better than being hunted by me. Your father pays well for me pursuing you. I intend to collect on this contract." Hector lies, trying to open the line of communication with Jensen.

"Well Hector, I have a problem with that." Jensen shifts, speaking with his cigar firmly pressed in his lips. His hand buried in his trench coat tightens as he firmly grabs six bullets.

"What problem do you have with that Jensen? It's a guarantee at life." Hector's palm begins to sweat lightly.

"Well, I know you're fucking lying." Jensen quickly tosses six polished silver bullets into the air as he swings his revolver out from behind him. The revolver pops open, spinning rapidly. The silver bullets hover in the air, tumbling end over end.

Jeff and James squeezed the triggers of their respective Berettas firmly as they projected hollow point, copper tipped rounds towards Jensen. With each squeeze, a light puff of smoke formed a haloed haze around the muzzle. Hector slowly pulled back the hammer of his revolver, keeping a firm lock on Jensen. Hector slides his index finger behind the trigger guard, exhaling as he pulls firmly on the trigger. A thick puff of smoke explodes out of the barrel encasing the muzzle as a single projectile pointed copper round shoots out towards Jensen. Jensen spins to his left, his trench coat flails wildly with this motion. Hollow point bullets shred through the thick trench coat and pierce into the glass of the building behind him. The larger round fired from Hector's revolver slices right above Jensen's left ear, shaving a few hairs before shattering the glass pane, creating a waterfall of glass behind him. Jensen spins back towards the right, his revolver still pointed downward. The tumbling silver rounds fall carefully in the cylinder. Jensen quickly snaps his wrist; the spinning cylinder locks into the revolver. He smacks the hammer rapidly with his free hand and a single silver round explodes with a flash of orange fire emitting out from the barrel of the gloss black revolver. A thick puff of white smoke emits from the cylinder as it cycles for the next round. The bullet slices through Jeff's left quad muscle, exiting quickly. Blood, flesh and muscle exit the wound behind the silver bullet. Blood from Jeff speeds off as the round smashed into a glass pane behind Hector and the twins. The glass explodes into a thousand shards and falls rapidly to the ground behind them.

Jeff drops onto his unwounded leg and continues to fire. James cautiously moves as he fires round after round. Thick smoke from the gunfight fills the enclosed atrium. Hector pulls the trigger as he fires another round in the direction of Jensen. Jensen spins back towards his left, locking his sights onto Jeff. He rapidly smacks the hammer back with the palm of his free hand before pulling quick and smooth on the trigger. The white handled revolver comes to life once again as smoke erupts from the cylinder. A short, bright orange flame expels another silver bullet from the muzzle. The round flies towards Jeff with accurate precision, striking him firmly through his neck, ripping a hole through his flesh, impacting the glass pane behind him, shattering it. The blood, flesh, and glass collapse into a mix on the ground. Jeff's eyes roll back as he his chest falls once and his massive frame collapses. James screams at the sight of his dead brother, charges at Jensen, keeping him in the Beretta's sights. His weapon bounces as his large frame strides across the atrium. James, firing as fast and wildly as the Beretta allows, closes the distance between Jensen and himself. Jensen stands his ground as the rounds fly off their mark into the building behind him. More glass explodes, causing millions of shards to fall harmlessly to the ground behind and around Jensen. Jensen, puffing his cigar, raises his revolver, smoke cascading down the barrel, lining James up in his sights. The silver bullet escapes, piercing through the skull of James Jeffcoat, exiting through the back of his head with a faint crack. Pieces of skull, brain and blood purse through the exit wound, as the lumbering giant falls forward, smacking the ground hard. Lifeless, it slides steadily to a stop; his head resting in front of Jensen boots, surrounding them in a viscous crimson liquid.

Hector cocks the hammer back, locking Jensen into his vision. Jensen slaps the hammer of his revolver back with the palm of his other hand, placing Hector square in his sights. The two men begin to slowly walk towards each other, locked firmly into the sights of their revolvers. Jensen's boots leave thin crimson prints as he crosses the atrium, moving closer to Hector. Hector breathes deeply as he approaches the man he's been chasing for so long. The two men stop a few feet from each other, their revolvers unwavering at the latest turn in the standoff.

"Hello Jensen, it's been a long time." Hector said, his soft voice carrying in the air.

"I'm sorry about Maria, but she had been turned. She was going to kill me." Jensen replies through his lips, lightly inhaling and exhaling another hit of his cigar.

"She turned a long time ago. Anna and Olivia are safe in the prison. We should really get going before Henry gets back with his gun. I'd hate to see that kid have to die today." Hector carefully releases his hammer as he brings his revolver down into his side holster. Jensen nods as he does the same.

"You know this alters our plans a bit Edmund." Jensen replies as he eliminates the few feet between them.

"I know, but it was getting to hard to keep these guys off your trail. They were the best the Department trained after all." Edmund explained as they slowly exit the atrium on the opposite side from where Jensen's apartment was located. As they leave, Henry walks reenters the atrium, amazed at the death and destruction from the gunfight. He races through the atrium to the opposite side and dives into the bushes. He watches Edmund and Jensen walk side by side away from the complex of glass buildings.

Chapter 11

Ambrose stood looking out through his glass sphere office high atop the Department of Time Justice. As the sun began its descent below the horizon, the lights from the office turned on; slowly growing brighter as the sun set further down, gently disappearing as darkness encapsulated the city below. Ambrose turned, his hands clasped behind his back.

"I wonder how Maria has fared. She should have been calling me by now." Ambrose paced worriedly, an unsettling pain in his heart, waiting for his phone to ring, hoping Maria would come and tell him the good news in person.

Ambrose stopped momentarily looking at his phone sitting on his desk, nothing was there. Each second that ticked by on the antique grandfather clock was a minor prick of a needle deep down.

"Maybe I should call her. Hector should be there too. I trust them, I know they will get it done, but what if something went wrong?" Ambrose's thoughts raced with excitement and terrifying fear that the worst had happened.

"I may have to get more firepower, more technology, and more money. Hector has come so close before, perhaps I have severely underestimated Jensen. He is my blood after all. No, impossible. I am the one that discovered time warps. I am the one that pioneered time travel and teleportation. I am the one with the destiny. I am the prophet of Apache. There is no other. Is there?"

His clasped hands begin to sweat as the clock continued it slow, torturous movement, putting Ambrose in a state of uneasiness. He rubbed his back as pacing quickened. He stopped in front of a tall bookcase next to the old grandfather clock, scanning the spines, hoping to find something to distract him from the silence of his office and his mind.

"Mr. Ambrose. Someone is on their way up to see you." A tender voice interrupts from a small black intercom box sitting on his desk.

"Alright Maggie, I'm up here. Who is it?" Ambrose casually replied. There is no response from the intercom. *"She's a good secretary, but sometimes I wish she would be better."* Ambrose chuckled, for a moment his mind free from the torture of waiting.

He walks to his desk, taking a seat, sliding open a small drawer on his left. He pulls out an old wood and steel flintlock pistol, a small cotton sack of gunpowder and a single lead ball. Carefully, he measures out a load of gunpowder using a small metal spoon within the sack. He dumps the gunpowder in through the small barrel. Grasping the redwood handle, he carefully places a small cotton patch across the barrel, and then gently slides the lead ball down the barrel. Gingerly sliding the packing rod out from under the barrel, he firmly presses onto the ball ensuring the lead round is packed tight. Cautiously, he pours a little more gunpowder into the pan, slowly closing the frizzen down on top of it. Ambrose raises the redwood pistol, using his thumb to slowly pull back on the hammer.

There is a ding from the high tech elevator outside his office and the floor at the opposite end of the spherical office opens. Ambrose looks straight down the barrel of the pistol as the lift rises into place.

"Jesus Christ Henry! I almost shot you!" Ambrose carefully sets the flintlock into the drawer as he stands up to greet Henry, who is covered in sweat and struggling to catch his breath.

"Boss, oh shit boss. We need to talk. We really need to talk. We have a major problem on our hands. I saw some stuff." Henry gasps.

"Ok, ok. Take your time Henry. Jesus, what happened? Where is Maria? Hector? And the twins? You look like you've seen a ghost." Ambrose minds whirls at the possibilities of why Henry, not Maria, and not Hector is standing before him. Henry bends at the waist, sucking in as much air as he can.

"Ambrose." Henry pauses rising back up. "We have a huge problem on our hands now. There was a gunfight. Blood everywhere! Maria's body." Henry paused again, this time his stomach turned with the image in his head and the smell of a singed corpse still deep in his nostrils. "Hector and Jensen, I saw them walk away together. Something isn't right boss. I think Hector changed sides. The twins are dead, so much blood, and glass everywhere." Henry was slowly regaining his breath. Ambrose was mystified by the broken story that Henry was trying to tell him.

"Henry, I need you to calm down. I need to know exactly what happened. Where is Maria? A gunfight, our Time Police would have heard that on their scanners. Henry, you aren't making any sense. Take a moment and calm down. Then tell me exactly what happened." Ambrose tries to piece together the broken information and get Henry to tell his story straight. Henry looks around the office as he takes a few more deep breaths.

"This is a nice office boss." Ambrose looks around, nodding.

"I know Henry. Can you please focus for a minute and tell me what happened?" Ambrose said dismissively.

"Oh yeah, you aren't going to like this at all. First, we positioned ourselves outside Jensen's apartment. We waited there for until well past when Maria was to have finished him off. Maria never came out, but Jensen did. We waited for him to walk off and then went up to the apartment on Hector's orders. I'm sorry boss, but he killed her. She's dead. Maria is dead, there isn't much left of her, oh God and the smell was bad." Ambrose raised his hand, cutting off Henry. Ambrose places his hand across his chest; as a small pain passes through his body. He sighed heavily as he puts his hand back down.

"Please, continue Henry. What else happened?" Henry looks oddly at Ambrose as he continues.

"So, we leave the apartment. We follow him to this atrium and there he is, against a tree; just waiting for us to find him. It's like he knew we were coming the entire time. There was a standoff;

it lasted a few minutes before I ran back to the van to get my sidearm. The gunfight started and all I could hear was glass shattering and gunfire. When I got my sidearm, everything went silent; I ran back and saw Jensen and Hector, leaving the atrium, together, like friends. I dove into some bushes to make sure, I am dead certain of what I saw."

Ambrose stepped back in disbelief. *How could he betray me? I've employed Hector for years; we'd been in this together for years. This can't be.* Ambrose seethed with contempt. *Jensen has stepped up his efforts. No more games. It's time I take care of this problem child myself.* Ambrose turned away from Henry.

Henry takes a few steps into the office and looks out through the glass sphere. Small lights dot the vast darkness of Apache. The city, seemingly at peace offered up no disturbance from the earlier gunfight, no usual activity of hover cars or nightclubs that typically light up the darkness.

Ambrose at his desk leans over to press a small button, revealing a bright holographic display. He frantically begins sliding through screens, each one disappearing into nothingness until he finally comes across the one he's looking for. *Time Department Citizen Monitoring Security Access Program.*

"Access name: Ambrose James, password: M-4-R-1-4." Ambrose barks, waiting for the screen to move.

"Access granted. Which camera would you like to monitor?" The holographic display replied. He pauses, looking through the translucent screen at

Henry. "Playback, Four Corners Condos, play the atrium film."

Henry steps behind Ambrose, watching. The access screen disappears as a live feed from the early morning plays. A figure in a trench coat and cowboy hat appears, strolling through the atrium, taking up a spot underneath a bent over willow tree. Ambrose watches intently as the screen unfolds exactly as Henry explained. The display shows Jensen and Hector walking side by side out of the atrium. Ambrose slams his hands on the desk, rising up furiously. Henry backs away quickly, startled by his reaction.

"Henry, did you ever notice anything strange about Hector? Did you notice any suspicious activity, sneaky phone calls, or meetings, anything like that?" Ambrose turned towards Henry stepping closer to where the redwood flintlock pistol rested. Henry trembling with fear shook his head.

"It's okay Henry. I know you wouldn't have let this occur if you would have known about this. You can relax. I'm just trying to figure out what Jensen could have offered Hector to betray me." Ambrose turns to look through the glass as the small lights flicker.

"There, there is one thing." Henry steps up next to Ambrose. "At the prison, there was a weak and sickly old man. I believe they called him Edmund. He was a spitting image of Hector. Hector interviewed him alone; he had the twins beat him, pretty ruthlessly. I didn't think anything of the resemblance until now. You don't know if Hector had a brother or relative do you?" Ambrose smiled at Henry.

"Henry, I've said it once, I'll say it again, you're a damn genius. This explains so much. There is apparently much more to Hector Luna than you and I know." Ambrose slumps in his chair, interlocking his fingers, his mind racing over all his past interactions.

'It all makes sense now. How else could Jensen have eluded him all these years? He's been sabotaging me every step of the way. All this time I thought I was entrusting my old friend Hector in capturing Jensen, it's been that bastard Edmund all along." Ambrose leans forward in his chair, watching Henry.

"You've done me a great service Henry. I will make sure you are well rewarded."

"Thanks Boss, I made a commitment to the Department and I will honor it." Henry replied looking out the window at the twinkling lights of Apache.

Ambrose eyes Henry as he slowly rises out of his chair, holding the redwood pistol behind his back, and walks towards him

"It's a beautiful city Henry. Soon I will rule and the Department will be entrusted with the security of all the denizens in Apache. We're going to make the world a better place." Henry stops mid nod as Ambrose pulls the gun from behind his back and pushes it against the back of Henry's head.

"What, what are you doing?" Henry trembles as the barrel of pistol plants itself against the base of his skull.

"Henry, you have to understand, you've been working for a notorious outlaw for the last decade. While I appreciate your cooperation, the one thing you have to know is that I can't ever trust you." Henry's eyes widen with fear. He tries to plea for his life but his voice has left him. "Henry, trust is a motherfucker." Ambrose slides his finger to the trigger and he winks at Henry as their eyes meet briefly. The trigger glides back with the smooth pull of his finger. The hammer rocks forward carrying the flint striking into the frizzen. A small spark ignites the gunpowder in the pan. The gunpowder in the pan ignites shooting through the small hole in the side of the fling igniting the loaded gunpowder inside the barrel. *BANG*! A small explosion shoots out the side of the flint as the lead ball ejects out the other end. The lead round sears through Henry's brain exiting with a faint rip between his eyes. The round smacks into the glass with a loud crack as it rolls to the ground encased in blood. Henry drops to his knees, his face slides down the curved pane leaving a streak of blood. Ambrose stands, looking over Henry's body.

"Maggie, we need a clean-up crew here right away. I need a few officers and a hover tank ready to go tomorrow morning. Please program the prison as the destination." Ambrose turns back towards his desk. "Copy, request submitted." The intercom clicks off. Ambrose looks around his office. "I'll see you tomorrow old friend. " He smiles as he turns away from the lifeless Henry and then leaves his office.

Chapter 12

Ambrose ran his hands through his hair, slicking it back with a dollop of grease. He smiled at his reflection in the mirror, checking that his teeth gleamed in the light. *"Money."* He thought. Stacked around him in his bedroom are piles of clothes, binders, and boxes labeled *miscellaneous research.* Times had been tough for a few years. Yet with his latest discovery, he was being asked to speak to a lobby of scientists. He was being heralded as a genius, especially when he would toss on a suit and tie instead of his weathered white lab coat. Ambrose took care to keep his suit jacket clasped to his hips, tucking his arms to his sides, stepping through the tiny space.

He walked cautiously towards the living room, passing photos of himself as a young scientist first followed by collages of college and high school photos with his friends. He barely glanced at them.

"It's been so many years of research. I don't even know what I should say." He was becoming unnerved with what he was being asked to present to scientists that he once looked up to. Ambrose walked into the living room where he encountered a young man and woman sitting patiently on the sofa.

"Ambrose! You look so professional. You clean up nice." The young woman stood and embraced him in a soft hug.

"Thank you Anna, my dear, this means so much to me. I'm so glad I have you and Edmund to share in this special moment with me." He spoke softly to Anna, returning her embrace. The young man stood up next as he made his way to Ambrose.

"I'm so proud of you. I've been alongside you on some of your research and this has been long overdue. I can't wait to hear your speech tonight. I know it will be motivational and inspiring for the entire community of scientists." He beamed a huge smile at Ambrose.

"Edmund, I owe a lot of this to you for encouraging and supporting my dedication to the time travel research through the years." The two men shook hands and exchanged smiles. "Well, I guess there is no time like the present. Let's get going." Ambrose made his way towards the front door. Edmund and Anna followed, quickly keeping pace with the excited scientist.

The three friends walked to a rust colored hatchback car that sat in the street. The smell of raw, rusted metal emanated from the car. Ambrose swung the driver door open exposing the torn leather seats with warped foam imprints to the warm air. A warm, musky odor met his nostrils causing him to take a step back.

"You guys think I'll be able to trade this in and get something a couple years newer?" He chuckled as he tenderly maneuvered into the seat being careful to adjust his suit so it didn't touch the exposed foam. Edmund opened the passenger door, stepping back as the musk escapes from the rusty car. Edmund reached down tilting the seat forward.

"Well my sweet, front or back?" He turned, smiling at Anna. Anna smiled, rolling her eyes.

"Front, my dress cost more than your little rented penguin suit." Edmund chuckled as he stepped timidly into the car, plopping down onto the flat back seat.

"Ouch, no padding," said Anna as she pushed the seat back to the upright position. Ambrose turned the key and the little rust bucket coughed and sputtered as the engine struggled to life. He grabbed the gear selector and muscles it down into drive. The car whirred as it shifted into gear. The little hatch lurched forward and began to hum along as they headed to the auditorium for Ambrose's speech.

Two large spotlights shot into the sky, their bright lights stretching into the night sky reaching towards the stars. The rusted little hatch halted in front of a sharply dressed valet. His fedora was as bright red as his jacket as he put his hand on the passenger door handle. Anna giggled as the young valet he shook the handle and pulled on the door with force. The door flung open knocking him backward, causing him to stumble on the nearby curb.

"Oh, be careful, we need it to stay together for the ride home sweetie." The valet carefully dusts off his jacket, regaining his composure. Anna gracefully exits as Edmund pushes the seat forward. Edmund stumbles out from the backseat, tripping over the curb. Ambrose muscles his door open as the car sputters, struggling to keep its motor running. The valet walks quickly around the front of the car, handing Ambrose a small blue ticket.

"Be careful kid, she may not look like much but it's a real beast once you sit behind the wheel." He explained, making his way to his waiting friends. The trio walks briskly up the stairs of the building, between the spotlights, and into the building.

"Ladies and gentleman, welcome to the first annual science awards night. We have spared no expense for tonight's festivities, to honor local scientific mastermind, Ambrose James. We have chosen to reward Ambrose for his perseverance, dedication, and ultimately his breakthrough in the field of time travel. We have hundreds of his peers here to recognize this astounding breakthrough in science and technology. So without further ado, enjoy your dinner while we prepare the stage for the award ceremony." A suave older man spoke; his white and black tuxedo matching his exquisitely combed hair. He waves out to the crowd as a mild applause courses through the auditorium. Edmund and Anna take seats directly in front of the podium. Ambrose walks behind them placing his hands on their backs.

"I've got to go to the back and prepare for my speech and ceremony. I'll see you guys after the big presentation." He quickly disappears into the crowd.

"Excuse me; I'm here to do the ceremony rundown." Ambrose approaches the man donned

In the white tuxedo, gently tapping him on his shoulder. The white tuxedo turns around to face Ambrose.

"Ambrose James. I have been so excited to meet you since hearing about your amazing discovery." White tuxedo extends his hand to Ambrose.

"Oh, you know who I am already. I guess my luck has changed." Ambrose quips, grabbing the stranger's hand in a firm handshake.

"Oh, not just me, I have a few friends who also know of you and your discovery. We can get to the ceremony in a few minutes, that part won't take long, but I'd really like to speak with you privately for a few if you care to join me for a little pre-ceremony drink?" He breaks the handshake tucking his hand into the front pocket of his tuxedo jacket.

"Well, as long as it's your treat. I'm sorry, but I didn't catch your name," said Ambrose.

"Oh, my apologies, I'm Wayne Clayton, President of Latentech. Until your breakthrough, we were considered the foremost experts in the research of time travel." Wayne shoots a crooked smile towards Ambrose.

"Ah, Mr. Clayton, you know you guys denied my application for a job a few years back. I'm willing to bet you regret that decision right now." He returns his verbal jab with a slight wink. Mr. Clayton chuckles and motions Ambrose to walk with him to the bartender. Ambrose follows warily.

The bartender tosses a maroon bottle in the air catching it smoothly behind his back, raising it to the small shot glasses set on the glossy marble bar. Wayne and Ambrose lean over the lip of the bar.

"You were right about Latentech regretting our human resource department's gross negligence in reviewing your application. The moment we heard you had potentially discovered the formula for time travel; the information was quickly up-channeled to me that we had missed out on hiring such a dedicated scientist. We like to think we hire the best and we obviously missed out." Wayne explained as he sips on the thickened red alcohol in his glass. Ambrose shifts uneasily against the bar.

"Are you just trying to give me the job I know longer want Wayne? Because I'm not interested," Ambrose downs his glass in one swig glares in contempt at Wayne.

"Oh no, I figured that ship had sailed. I am here to offer you something though. I think you won't be able to refuse it." Wayne polishes off his drink in one motion.

"Well, Mr. Clayton, sir, you definitely have my attention now." Ambrose motions for another round. Wayne places his hand sternly on Ambrose's shoulder.

"We did some research into your past research and personal life once we heard about your discovery. What if I told you that with Latentech funding, and your discovery, you could become the richest, most powerful man in the world? I'm pretty sure that would go a long way in helping persuade young Anna to choose you and not Edmund." Ambrose looks at the hand on his shoulder.

"You know Mr. Clayton; I have spent my life to this point doing everything I thought I could to persuade Anna to be with me. What exactly are you proposing?" Ambrose asks.

"Ambrose, I'm proposing to you to let Latentech, not only build your time travel device, but aid you in forming an all-powerful, rich government, that will control every aspect of time travel. With your technology we could change the past so that your future is very lucrative, both professionally and personally." Wayne stood, adjusting his tux.

"Well, Wayne, I wouldn't mind change my status in the world." The two men shake hands firmly as they make their way back to the auditorium.

"Ladies and gentlemen, it is time for our award presentation followed by a speech from our awardee Ambrose James." Wayne spoke into the microphone. "Latentech has always prided itself on being industry leading, and entrepreneurial in all aspects of scientific research and development. That doesn't mean we are always the best folks suited for the job. As we celebrate Ambrose James, for his dedication to his research in the field of time travel, we are more than honored to award him with the first ever Latentech Prestige Medal. We got together with some of our competitors looking for the best and brightest innovations from the last year and it was unanimous. We had to award Ambrose James this very distinguished medal for the scientific research community. This medal is probably not as prestigious as Ambrose's amazing discovery to our close knit community, but it is going to serve as the dawning of a new era for Apache. As our scientific community bolsters here within the city, Ambrose and his discovery will be forever etched in the annals of history as the single most important discovery of our time. Ambrose James, please join me on stage and accept your medal." Wayne turns to his left, clapping loudly. Edmund and Anna lead the raucous standing ovation that echoes and reverberates inside the walls. Ambrose walks from behind the curtain, crossing the stage as he waves his hands out to the adoring masses.

"Thank you all. I mean it, from the bottom of my heart. I am so very honored that my peers and scientific community, some of whom I've looked up to for the better part of my young life are her in attendance to honor me. Thank you, Mr. Clayton, for everything you have done for this community as President of Latentech. I'd like to start off by thanking the two people who encouraged and pushed me, continuously to keep my research going. Anna, Edmund, you are the best friends any person could ask for, thank you. Now, time travel has always fascinated me. Being able to go back in history and see events live as they unfold. I imagine a world where our children can go back in history and see history unfold, learn in real time how these events shaped our city, our country, our world. I hope that with further research, this can not only better us as a whole society, but increase the net worth of the individual knowledge that can be gained by studying our past. This is why I'm pleased to announce, that with Latentech funding, we will be developing the first time travel device to be tested with transporting a human through time."

Anna and Edmund looked at each other, stunned by Ambrose's announcement, while the rest of the auditorium continues their thunderous applause. Ambrose's smile beamed brighter than the spotlights outside.

"Thank you for your time. I did it guys!" He smiles pointing towards Anna and Edmund from behind the podium. Ambrose turns as Wayne puts his arm around his back. The two wave to the audience as they walk off the stage.

As people hurriedly file out of auditorium in droves, Edmund and Anna stand outside patiently as Ambrose walks up with Wayne Clayton.

"Hey Anna, Edmund, this is Wayne Clayton, President of Latentech.," said Ambrose introducing his friends.

"Pleased to meet you Mr. Clayton, you're helping out a very good and dedicated scientist further his research." Edmund extends his hand. Mr. Clayton looks down at it and then at Anna.

"I hope you two don't mind, but I'm going to be stealing Ambrose for a little further celebration back at Latentech. I trust you have a ride back." Edmund puts his hand at his side as Ambrose pulls the blue valet ticket out of his pocket.

"Would you guys mind taking the rust bucket back to the house? I don't want to have to find my way back here to pick it up." Anna grabs the ticket quickly.

"Ambrose, be careful. We will get your car back, if you need anything call Edmund and he will come get you." Her voice betrays her worry.

"Don't worry Anna; he will be perfectly happy with Latentech." Wayne interjects, putting his arm around Ambrose. "Come my new genius friend, we have some fun waiting for us." Wayne and Ambrose saunter down the stairs to a waiting limousine. Edmund and Anna trail them to watch on their dear friend. Wayne enters the limo first. Ambrose turns waving once to his friends as he climbs in next to Wayne. Edmund and Anna wave halfheartedly. The limousine pulls away as the couple watches it drive off.

"I don't think I like this Anna." Edmund turns to her. "Ambrose is a good guy; he'll be fine, right?" Worried lines etch her face. Edmund embraces her tightly, gently kissing her forehead.

"Right," Edmund replied, unsure of Ambrose's future.

Chapter 13

The limousine weaves in and out of traffic as the reflecting glares of streetlights and car headlights dash across the deep tint of the windows. Ambrose occasionally checks the window to ensure his ride isn't about to be impaled by another vehicle or worse. He glances over to Mr. Clayton, who is gingerly sipping on a red liquid, cascaded with ice. With each evasive swerve of the limo, Clayton emits a boisterous chuckle. Ambrose clutches his hands on the edge of the faux leather seat, digging his nails underneath the embroidered piping.

"Relax Ambrose. We're going to have a good time and then we're going to discuss your future with Latentech. For now, enjoy the ride, your night is just beginning." Clayton tosses a clear bottle filled with red liquid at Ambrose; it lands harmlessly in his lap.

"Pour yourself one; it'll take the edge off." He chuckles again; the wheels on the limo lock up as it slides into a sharp left turn. Ambrose grabs a glass from the nearby drink console, lifting the lid to access the ice compartment. He scoops the ice into the glass, placing it carefully between his legs. The limo sharply turns throwing Ambrose against the door. Ambrose rolled his shoulder and twisted the lid.

The red liquid had a pungent odor. Ambrose tilted his glass in one hand, carefully bringing the neck of the bottle to rest as the liquid oozes into the glass, slithering down around the ice cubes. He fills it more than halfway before capping the bottle and tosses it back to Clayton. Ambrose whisks the cubes, thinning the red liquid. Repulsed by the odor, he takes a quick sip, the red liquid igniting a flame in the back of his throat.

"It'll burn any disease right of you. Special home brew, 90% alcohol, I call it Claymore. Like the mines from the old war days. So potent, it'll blow you up from inside." Clayton smiles as Ambrose gags down another sip.

"I can't feel my face." Ambrose quips. The two men laugh as the limo screeched to a halt, trying to maintain contact with the street.

The limo driver opens the door and Ambrose slinks out, holding his drink in both hands. Mr. Clayton follows, carrying his bottle of Claymore at his waist. The limo has come to a halt outside a high reaching skyscraper. Clayton adjusts his belt around his waist as he saunters towards a doorman standing guard of the slick, sliding glass doors.

"This isn't Latentech. We've arranged a wonderful private party for you at one of my penthouse suites. You're a damn scientific rock god Ambrose. I'm going to show you how you should be living your life tonight." The doorman opened the door, bowing his head at Clayton and Ambrose. Inside of the luxurious marble lobby, a large white fountain with three jumping, white marble dolphins, is centered at the large sitting area. Ambrose looks around, awestruck at the elaborate architecture falling behind Clayton.

"Come on young man. You can come down here any time you want and look at stuff. It's not good for a guest of honor to be late to their own party." Clayton hurries, still clutching his bottle of Claymore. Ambrose takes a deeper swig of his glass, which goes down smoother. He can feel himself relaxing. Ambrose lunges into the elevator after Mr. Clayton.

"Almost lost you there," Clayton puts his arm around Ambrose. The elevator doors chime as it begins it gradual ascent towards one of the penthouse floor suites.

The elevator chimes as it rustles to a stop and the doors slide open. The penthouse suite is illuminated with flashes of laser lights and strobes beating repeatedly across the walls and windows. Loud pumping music shakes the floor as hundreds of people dance with drinks in hand, bumping and grinding the night away. Clayton steps out ahead of Ambrose and raises his hands, causing the lights to come on, and exposing raunchy behavior. A small man, dressed like a bellboy, rushes up placing a microphone into Clayton's free hand. Clayton takes a swig from the bottle of Claymore as everyone stares at him. A few of the raucous couples have paused mid-intercourse, awaiting Clayton to speak.

"Ladies and Gentleman, I already know you're having a fantastic evening, but it's about to get crazy. I have in the elevator behind me, the next big thing. Some of you may want to call him Father Time because of his breakthrough in time travel technology. Some of you ladies may want to call him daddy, and some of you gentlemen may want to do the same, but I can do you all one better. I call him Ambrose; he is the newest acquisition by Latentech. He's a fucking science rock star. Ladies and gentleman, say hello to Father Time himself, Ambrose James!" Clayton shouts, and turns, applauding Ambrose. Ambrose takes a swig of Claymore and walks across the elevator threshold. A deafening noise erupts inside the penthouse. The lights flick back off as the bass of the music pulsates through the floor. Clayton grabs Ambrose's hand and raises both their arms high above their heads.

"I told you. You're a damn hero around here." He grins again. A wave of elation surged through Ambrose. The two men walk down two short steps and they are immediately surrounded by a throng of drunken degenerates, whooping and hollering.

Clayton releases Ambrose's arm as they high five and hug the random masses of people, fighting through the crowd to get a chance to meet the Latentech man of the hour. Women walk up, baring everything god and plastic surgery has given them. They embrace and molest him, occasionally grabbing his hand and rubbing it across their massive, silicon infused, bosoms. Some of the men even guide Ambrose to a handful of their virility. Clayton reaches back, pulling Ambrose by the shirt, helping to guide him through the crowd towards and empty sitting booth.

Clayton motions Ambrose to slide in first, sliding in next to him. The booth is covered in a firm leather cushion and curves around a white marble table that has a stainless steel pole shooting straight from its center and attaching to the ceiling.

"This is insane. None of my friends would ever believe a company could value science and scientists so much." Clayton chuckles at Ambrose's admission.

"Son, none of your friends even matter now. You're a Latentech man now. Everything you see here can be yours whenever you need it. Anything you can ever imagine needing. Funding? Done. New equipment? Done. Women, men, dogs, cats, and alcohol. You think of it Ambrose, and I'll make sure you have it." Ambrose is taken aback by the frankness of Clayton's offerings, as two voluptuous women walk onto the table. They begin a seductive enchantment twirling and sliding around the stainless steel pole. Ambrose watches on in amazement while Clayton pours more Claymore into two new glasses for himself and Ambrose.

Minutes erode away into hours as the party vibrates around them. Ambrose gets lap dances and makes out with a few random women who make their way to his table. Clayton goes out of his way to ensure Ambrose has more than enough attention and entertainment as they relax in the immense party atmosphere of the penthouse.

"So what do you think Ambrose? Latentech has already made you a rock star. How would you feel about working with me and not for me?" Clayton asks, shooing away the groupies.

"I thought you said we would talk about this after the party?" Ambrose, drunk, manages to slur out.

"Ambrose, my boy, Latentech is one big party. We bring you onboard and the majority of our work is done. There are some small things I would need you to do for me, but I can guarantee you anything you could ever want. Money, fame, power, anything you want that's all at our disposal Ambrose. I have never extended this to anyone, but I have some robust plans for Apache and I want you to be my figurehead." Clayton slides next to Ambrose placing his arm around him and points his finger at his chest. "You could become the most powerful man in Apache."

Ambrose turns his head towards Mr. Clayton. "I don't know if it's the amount of alcohol or all the women fawning over me, but I like the sound of that." Ambrose burps softly. Clayton releases his arm leaning back chuckling.

"I get it, I got you. We can discuss this when we get freshened and sobered up. Enjoy the night Ambrose. Everything here is here because we want you here. I want you here with Latentech. We can change the world with your help. Enjoy the night, my boy." Clayton pats Ambrose on the back and slides out of the booth as a young woman slides on the opposite side of Ambrose, her breasts pressed against his arm. Ambrose looks at her and back towards Clayton. He raises his hand in a half attempt at waving a good-bye. The young woman quickly maneuvers onto his lap, drawing all of his attention towards her.

An intense brightness pierces through his eyelids. Ambrose rolls over, finding himself in a strange bed. The mattress is firm; the pillows and comforter are plush and bury him in a sea of soft white cotton. He pushes his way off the massive bed, shielding his eyes from the blinding light sneaking through long vertical blinds. He rubs his hands across his chest, as he realizes he is only wearing briefs. He turns to see the young woman who he vaguely remembers meeting, lying peacefully under the comforter, obviously naked. Ambrose, ashamed, quickly walks out to investigate the penthouse. He hurries through a short hallway and into the room where party had taken place. There wasn't a single trace of debauchery. The penthouse had been thoroughly cleaned and had been completely rearranged into a respectable living area. Stomach growling, Ambrose made his way into the kitchen, where a note lay on the gleaming counter.

To Ambrose:

I hope you enjoyed the night. Miranda elected to keep an eye on you until you recover. Treat her right. She's one of my best secretaries and doesn't typically come to our parties. She really wanted to meet you when she heard I was trying to acquire you and your skills. The penthouse is yours. It's completely stocked with food and drinks. A maid service will clean it daily. We can talk about your contract this afternoon.

Take Care,

Big C

Ambrose returns the note and begins to sift through the kitchen gathering eggs, bacon and orange juice to prepare breakfast. He pauses at the plates and takes two down when Miranda walks into the kitchen, wearing a white terry bath robe. After an awkward silence, Miranda speaks.

"Look, I'll go. We don't need to make this awkward. We were both really out of it last night."

Miranda, embarrassed by her actions, speaks timidly. Ambrose lets out a sigh but leaves both plates down.

"I'd like for you to stay." He says, sitting next to her at the countertop bar. During the next few hours, they discuss everything, finally agreeing on a date for the night after Ambrose meets with Clayton. Ambrose can't believe his luck.

Zooming through traffic, screeching brakes and the body roll of the limo as it narrowly avoids smashing into other cars. Sitting in the limo, Ambrose takes a few deep breaths, confident in the limo driver's ability. He knows Latentech wants him and he can feel they will give him anything he needs to be the best scientist he can be. He's also never had as much fun with a prospective employer as he did last night, not to mention, there's a beautiful woman that is interested in him because of his intelligence. Ambrose ponders the possible pros and cons of working for Latentech but he can't get Mr. Clayton's words out of his head. The more Ambrose thinks about it, the more he wants to be 'the most powerful man in Apache.' The limo stops in front of the Latentech campus.

The campus is a sprawling white building that stretches for thousands of feet. Deep tinted windows line every floor and stretch as far as the eye can see. Ambrose takes a few strides when he hears a familiar voice greeting him.

"Good morning. Hope you enjoyed the night. Welcome to Latentech." Mr. Clayton smiled thrusting his hand into Ambrose's.

"Well, I woke up next to a gorgeous woman who wants to go have a romantic dinner with me, so I'd say I had a really great night."

Clayton chuckles, slapping Ambrose on the back, "Nope, Miranda's been really interested in you since she heard me mention you might be coming on board. I think she likes that whole nerdy scientist thing you have going." He motions Ambrose to follow him.

The two men walk through the campus stopping periodically at different departments to meet each of the lead scientists. At the end of the tour, Clayton brings him to his office, in a large glass atrium at the end of the building. Bookcases occupy the atrium, some with scientific books, some with trophies and awards, forming a narrow pathway to an open area with a glass desk and two chairs. Clayton motions for Ambrose to take a seat and he glides into his chair.

"Look these over," Clayton said, sliding a contract packet towards him and turning to the computer. Clayton wasn't joking around; Latentech really wanted him to work there. Scanning through the contract, Anderson gives a little nod.

"Got a pen?" The old man doesn't look up from his tasks and flicks a silver pen across the table.

"I do just have one question. This contract doesn't mention how you're going to help make me the most powerful man in Apache." Ambrose leans back in the chair, leaving the pen on the table.

"Very astute young Ambrose, those details you and I will draw up at a later date." Clayton stares hard at him, willing him into signing.

"No. That's not going to work. You got me interested by promising these things, and that one thing in particular is what would seal the deal for me. Let's change the world together." Ambrose sets the contract back on the table, still unsigned. Clayton pivots his chair, giving him his undivided attention.

"With my money and ideas, I want to create a Time Justice Department." Clayton describes an enforcement agency that travels in time to prevent crimes from happening, once they've already happened. "Where you come in my dear Ambrose, is that with your discovery we can make this happen. In return, not only will you head this Department of Time Justice, but we will use it to oust the incumbent Mayor of Apache for not wanting to protect the citizens. That opening, that title, Mayor of Apache, will be all yours Ambrose, if you sign the contract today."

Mr. Clayton clasps his hands together and rests them on the table. Ambrose leans forward and squiggles his name onto the contract.

"If you'll excuse Me., I have really beautiful woman on her way to my penthouse. I'll start bringing my research over tomorrow." The two men smile and shake firm on their agreement.

"Once again my boy, enjoy the night." Clayton bids Ambrose goodbye as he left for his romantic rendezvous with Miranda.

Chapter 14

Edmund Jima stood in front of a table of two men and one woman, in white lab coats, with small ID badges, hung from the right breast pocket. While he couldn't make out the sets of numbers or names, he could, however, easily see the unknown logo. An A, formed by two assault rifles tilted so that the barrels touched to form the stems of the letter. The magazines curved, overlapping, forming the intersection at the mean line. He squints, trying to focus on the writing written in an unknown language at the bottom of the badge, focusing solely on the male figure seated in the middle.

"Mr. Jima," the figure in the middle finally speaks in a deep voice. "Do you know why you are here?" Edmund stops squinting, taken aback at finally being addressed by the panel of figures in front of him.

"No. I don't even know where I am. I don't know who you are or why you brought me here. You are the ones who brought me here right?" He asked. The female off to the right, leans in slightly, placing her arms across the table.

"Mr. Jima, what is your relationship with Ambrose James?" Her Russian accent grinds on his ears.

"What do you know of Mr. James and his research? Do you know his current whereabouts? When was the last time you have seen Ambrose? What role did you play in his research?" As she rattles off questions, Edmund wipes his sweaty palms across his khakis.

126

"I, I haven't seen Ambrose in almost a year. The last time I saw him he was getting into a limousine with Wayne Clayton. I don't know where he went after that. They were going to celebrate his discovery and partnership with Latentech. Anna and I, we had a weird, uneasy feeling about it. We took his car back from the auditorium and he never came back. Unfortunately, I don't know anything about his research, all I did was encourage him to keep working on it, and he never disclosed his work or discoveries. He was my best friend, he still is, I think." Edmund trails off, waiting for a response.

The trio whisper. He strains, trying to make out a word or two.

"Mr. Jima, perhaps, we aren't asking the right questions. What is your relationship with Anna? Do you know where we might be able to find her so we can ask her some questions?" The male figure in the middle of the table spoke again, leaning in slightly, his stubble and tinted goggles becoming more defined.

"Anna? Why do you need Anna?" Edmund asks uneasily. The older man leans to his right, whispering to the other male, who has yet to speak. The trio shifts uneasily.

"Look, I don't know where I am, who you are, or what you want with me. I will not say anything more unless you answer the questions I have." Edmund angrily spoke. A chair slides back, the metal legs screeching across the concrete floor.

Edmund stiffens as he hears heavy footsteps on his left. In a moment, a young man with a jet black goatee greets him warmly. Edmund astonished takes a step back.

"Hector! Brother, where, how, what's going on?" The twins stare at each other for a moment before the two embrace each other in a hug. They slowly break the embrace giving each other the once over.

"I'm going to tell you what's going on Edmund, but I need to know that you are going to help us get Anna, she's in great danger. We're trying to get her to safety before Ambrose gets to her." Hector places his hands on his brother's shoulders. Edmund tenses and Hector drops them.

"The two people behind me are Mr. Alec Ovila and Dr. Tasha Rilanov; they are former scientists with Latentech, as am I. We were part of Mr. Clayton's time travel research team for many years. Unfortunately, we only got to work with Ambrose his first week at Latentech before we discovered what Mr. Clayton and Ambrose were actually up to. We were unceremoniously removed from Latentech and forced into hiding, so that we couldn't let the public know what was going on in the research department. Ambrose and Mr. Clayton are going to use this technology to change the world, but not like we anticipated. They're starting to train teams of time cops to travel through time and alter their own individual history so that they can take over Apache and rule it and eventually the rest of the world. They are absolutely up to no good. I know Ambrose wants to go back and prevent Anna from ever meeting you. He wants to steal

Anna away from you, from your life, from your memories. That's why you're here. We need to keep her safe and we can only do that with your help." Edmund shocked, stares confusedly at his brother. The story of Ambrose and Mr. Clayton seemingly bent on world domination doesn't sound like his friend.

"Why couldn't you just tell me? Why did you have to drag me away? I, I don't know if I can trust you. Why is this so veiled in secrecy brother?" Edmund angrily inquires.

"Listen Edmund, brother, we are putting ourselves at an enormous risk every time we step out of the shadows, but we can't do it ourselves. We had to get you somewhere safe so that we could bring you in our plan, on what we're trying to accomplish. We had hoped Anna would have been with you, but for the first time in the year we've been watching you, you weren't together when we made the move. Let me tell you what we, The Awakened are planning to accomplish." Hector replied calmly, sensing the conflicting thoughts.

Another metal chair slides roughly against the concrete floor. Slow, labored footsteps make their way towards Edmund, revealing Mr. Ovila, who limps up to the men.

"Edmund, I'm sorry for confusion, but we're getting information from our contacts inside that Ambrose is getting close to being able to teleport the first team of time cops back in time. This is why I brought you here; to help us awaken the citizens of Apache. We decided immediately after being chased out at Latentech, that we couldn't allow this to take place. It was not long after that, that we learned that you and Anna were in grave danger. Ambrose, he may have been your friend at one time, but he's been corrupted. Mr. Clayton has filled his mind with thoughts of overwhelming riches, power and what Ambrose has always wanted that he couldn't have. You're Anna. We don't have a lot of time to make sure she's safe. I need you to trust me. I need you to trust us." Edmund trying to decipher trust behind Mr. Olivia's tinted glasses glance down at the ID badge. He mouths the words "ad astra per aspera." Edmund looks up.

"What does that mean?" He asked.

"It means 'To the Stars through difficulties.' For us, The Awakened, it means no matter the trials, we can reach the stars. It's meant to motivate us in the face of an overwhelming, growing enemy that we will always be able to rise above their plight and succeed in our mission." Olivia explained, patting Edmund as he limps back to his seat.

"We're going to write everything down and then you and I will go get Anna. We will make sure she is safe Edmund. You and I; taking on the evil that have always, secretly, been behind Latentech." Hector smiles as he leaves his brother to join the others in the darkness.

Edmund breathes deeply, trying to get his thoughts in line.

"I, I want to keep Anna safe. I need to keep her safe. I couldn't do this without her; I can't do life without her. I, I have to trust these guys. I know I can trust Hector, he's my own brother. He wouldn't

130

have told me about Ambrose or gone out of his way to keep safe if there was anything suspicious about this group. I can't let Ambrose take her from me. I, I can't let anyone take her from me." Edmund squints into the darkness and pauses briefly before he speaks.

"Anna should be back at the house. We have been keeping an eye on Ambrose's abandoned house since we lost contact with him. That's where she was heading. I don't know how long you have had me here, but she should be back by now, if not, then you know where to look." A pen scribbles lightly, sliding slowly across a lone piece of paper sitting on the table in front of The Awakened.

"Thank you, brother. Open the door Gus. Take him to get some food and something to drink." Hector calls out as a door clicks open behind Edmund. The dark room fills with bright light from the hallway outside. "Go get something to eat. I'll finish things up here with Alec and Tasha and then come get you. Then, we will go make sure Anna is safe." A large hand grips Edmund on the shoulder and muscles Edmund out of the room.

Hector rises as the door shuts, facing his colleagues.

"What's on your mind, young Hector?" Alec asks as Hector stands, staring at the closed door.

"Mr. Ovila, Tasha, it's been a great honor working with scientific minds like yours over the past couple years. What you taught me at Latentech will always live on with me."

Tasha shifts in her seat uneasily. "What are you going on about Hector? You are still here with us.

131

We still have much work to do, much more to learn, much more to teach." Hector turns around, a deceptive, evil smile across his face.

"Money and power will be everything under the rule of Ambrose James." Hector slid his hands into his lab coat, drawing out two small pistols and aimed them at Alec and Tasha who grabbed each other before they slumped over from the bullets embedded in their brain, the name "Edmund," escaping their dying bodies.

Hector tossed the empty pistols at the slumped body and laughed as he exited the room. Gus, hidden in the shadow of the intersecting hallway, scurried back to the cafeteria to warn Edmund.

Gus runs in the cafeteria and immediately runs to Edmund, his lumbering, muscular frame knocking trays and people over.

"Edmund, you have to run. Now! Hector is Latentech. I saw their bodies. Run, Edmund, run and save Anna." His whispers hit Edmund full force, pain reflecting in his eyes. Edmund rises, dropping his silverware on the floor.

"Go, out the back, that way. I'll hold him up." Gus waves him towards the exit and runs to fortify the entrance. Edmund runs out and pushes through two doors and sprints down the hallway, only stopping to read a fire exit map, to find out the nearest exit. After a few minutes, a bright red sign beckoned at the end of a hallway. Faint muffled gunshots echo down the hallway as Edmund pushing on the heavy exit door, rushes out into the unknown.

Chapter 15

A light dust appeared against the soft, lush gently waving grass, as a lone black sedan traveled a winding dirt road towards a small church. The car barely kicks up any dust save for the occasional pebble from under the edge of the sidewall. As it continues towards the church, the occupants fail to notice the thickening dust beside the road.

The shape of a man emerges from the dust, starting with his black boots, followed by his black clothing, followed by the unmistakable outline of his trench coat and Stetson. Jensen James emerges, patting the dust from his clothing. He lightly dabs at his bleeding nose with a handkerchief.

"Fuck. You would think this would eventually stop, right Olivia?" Jensen turned, looking for his partner. "Olivia? Where the hell are you?" Jensen barks at the fading dust. Jensen steps to his left as Olivia emerges rapidly through the dust, tumbling across the grass and coming to a sudden stop, hitting the dirt road violently.

"Motherfucker! Why does that always happen? My face, my beautiful face," Olivia wails as Jensen shakes his head side to side.

"Get up goofball. I know you're fine." Jensen extends his hand, pulling her to her feet. "Wow, not even an 'are you okay?'

"Well, you know if you wouldn't do that every single time it happens to you when we go through the rift, I would probably be a little more concerned with your health and well-being."

"Thanks, you big, old, brawny asshole." Olivia pats her clothes contemptuously, big clouds of dust envelope her. Jensen watches intently, grinning from beneath the brim of his dusty black Stetson.

Olivia's red eyes take in the rolling hillside as she turns her attention toward the church on the top of the hill at the end of the winding dirt road.

"We don't have much time. We need to get to them before everyone else shows up. Do you think they'll believe us?" Olivia asks Jensen.

"I want them to believe us, will they? Probably not, but they are the ones that gave us those stupid pills to be able to make us time travel without teleport plates. So, we just kind of have to hope they believe us. I mean, they really kind of have to or they will be dead, and if they end up dead, well, then you end up dead." Jensen looks down at Olivia as starts they start to walk down the grassy hillside towards the church.

"You know we could just walk on the road Jensen that would be an acceptable approach instead of trying to shortcut up and down these hills through the grass." Olivia pushes on Jensen's arm lightly.

"We don't have time for a romantic stroll through the countryside Olivia. This is serious. If we don't tell Edmund and Anna about what Ambrose is going to try to do at their wedding you could disappear and be gone forever. Poof! No more Olivia, gone, dead, like you never existed. Unfortunately for you, you aren't going to get rid of me that easily." Jensen pushes Olivia sending her rolling down the hill a few feet.

"Damn it! You time outlaws sure know how to make a woman feel loved." Olivia pops back quickly as Jensen stops beside her; she puts her arm around his back. The two continue their path.

The black sedan halts at the entrance kicking up a small cloud of dust. Edmund and Anna step out shutting the doors behind them, looking at each other over the roof.

"Are you nervous?" Anna asks, rubbing her forearm.

"Of course I'm nervous; I'm not supposed to see you on the day we're getting married before you walk down the aisle. It's bad luck supposedly." Edmund laughed.

"Well, if we had come up here yesterday and set everything up we wouldn't be having this problem. We have a couple hours before our guests get here so we better get cracking." Anna walks to the trunk, staring down Edmund, who just stands staring that the sky.

"Edmund, get over here and open the trunk!" Edmund shuffles to the back of the car, keys jingling in his hand. Anna glares at him with her lips stretched in a thin line.

"Sorry." Edmund hangs his head as he slides the key and lifts the trunk up. Anna kisses his cheek softly as he shuffles around in the trunk, grabbing some of the wedding decorations in his hands.

"Sometimes I can't tell if you're really mad at me or if you are just being snarky." Edmund kisses Anna on the lips.

"Edmund, I'm always snarky, even when I'm really mad at you." Anna grabs two garment bags and drapes them over her arm the black sedan bouncing lightly as she shuts the trunk.

Walking towards the church, she immediately drops the garment bags, gasping with her hands over her mouth. Leaning against the church is a man in all black garb. She can't see his eyes, but Anna can feel them staring her down, piercing into her soul.

"Hello Anna," said he addresses her, raising his head.

Edmund saunters out of the small church, encountering the two of them, as a woman appears next to the trench coated, Stetson wearing figure. She turns her head and her red eyes lock onto Edmund. His stomach flutters as he feels devil red eyes searing his flesh and sucking his soul. Cautiously, Edmund returns to Anna's side, putting an arm around her waist, waiting on the strangers to speak.

"Edmund, Anna, it's been a little while." Jensen's right hand grips the tip of his hat, sweeping it off his head, kneeling in front of Anna. His stone gray eyes look up towards hers with a slight grin. Anna looks to Edmund and then back down at Jensen.

"Jensen?" Her eyes shoot next to the red eyed devil standing behind the kneeling Jensen.

"Olivia?" Tears escape her eyes as Edmund's arm slumps back to his side.

"How did you guys know to come back here? This is really dangerous for you to be here. We were warned by ourselves that you may be coming back to protect us from something. Is that what you are

doing here? We need to get inside so we can talk."
Anna disappears into the church tugging on
Edmund's sleeve, leaving Jensen and Olivia
outside.

"Well, I think that went well. They knew we
were coming and they didn't freak out and try to kill
you. Double bonus." Olivia exclaimed cheerfully
Jensen as he rises, placing his Stetson back onto his
head, tilting the front down over his brow. He
shakes his head at Olivia.

"You know, one day, I will be trying to save
you, because your mouth will have put us into a lot
of trouble," he quipped rolling his eyes, heading up
the steps of the church/ "Come on, we need to get
everything prepared so we can get back out of here.
Wouldn't want to really alter the course of our
futures by getting caught in an unexpected gunfight,
right?"

"I love how you rushed into how dangerous this
is without even letting me reply to your first
statement." Olivia laughed, placing her hands
lightly on his shoulders. He swings his arm behind
his back pulling her quickly around. Olivia tips the
brim of the Stetson up, her red eyes locking with
Jensen's gray stone irises. Her lips press lightly
against Jensen's cheek, her fiery red eyes linger in a
gaze with Jensen that feels like an eternity.

"We better get inside." Jensen replied coldly,
focusing on the mission.

Anna hangs purple and white streamers down
the rows of pews; while Edmund hangs large paper
flowers on each pew, carefully securing the flowers
on top of the decorations. Jensen sits on the ledge of

137

the stage, overlooking the rows of pews, impatiently tapping his fingers. Olivia runs her hands over the top of the pews, double checking streamers and flowers. Finished, she makes her way to the front of the church taking a seat next to Jensen. The purple and white pew decorations serve as a subtle contrast to the neon orange lantana's that adorn a few large vases sporadically though the church. Anna lifts up her bouquet, consisting of the same bright orange lantana's, off of a pew and carries it to the rear of the church. Edmund having finished with his task wipes his sweaty hands on his pants, as he leans against the first pew, his eyes racing.

"So, we already know why you're here. Well, I think we know." Edmund hesitates, looking at Anna, who has now walked up beside him. "Well, what we were told anyways is that you would be coming to warn us of our good friend Ambrose. So, while we haven't heard or seen from him in a couple years, we believe it's a good possibility that he has gone off course with his research. With that being said, nobody, not even Ambrose, has the knowledge or research of what happens if you interfere in the past." Edmund shifts, turning more towards Jensen. Anna interrupts, sensing Edmund's unease.

"I think Edmund is trying to say, let us know what he's bringing, and what we need to do to be able to survive or put a stop to this, and we'll do it. We don't want to run the risk of altering our future, or Olivia's." At the mention of her name, Olivia looks up towards Anna, feigning a smile. Jensen rises slowly in front of Edmund, tilting the Stetson down deep over his eyes. Jensen stares at the floor, not looking at Edmund.

"You're going to need guns, and bullets. Lots of guns, lots of bullets, and even then, you still won't have enough to stop the people that Ambrose is bringing. He wants you dead, he wants Anna to himself, and he wants to rewrite the history of his unrequited love. You stand no chance." Jensen paused. "I'll be on my way now." Jensen brushes past Edmund leaning against the pew, whose gut churns as his eyes meet with Anna's and then Olivia's.

"Well, Anna, Edmund, I guess I should be going as well. Need to keep an eye on the one man that is going to stop Ambrose someday." Olivia jumps up off the stage, hugging Anna tightly, glancing at her father. She walks up to Edmund, locking eyes.

"He won't let anything happen. I know he seems a little self-serving and rude, okay he's a lot of those things, but he will do whatever it takes to get a shot at Ambrose." Olivia leans up, kissing her father gently on the cheek, humming as she strolls out of the church. Edmund and Anna embrace, worry etched on their faces.

"Well, at least we have guns." Edmund kisses Anna's forehead tenderly.

Familiar faces of friends and family arrive in droves. Anna occasionally peaks out of her room in the rear of the church; her eyes scanning the crowd, warily, on the lookout for Ambrose.

Fidgeting at the altar, Edmund wipes his hands on the front of his pants, scanning the crowd.   A hand lands on Edmund's shoulder, startling him. Looking up, he can see into the stone gray eye of the priest, staring dead into his soul. The priest removes his hand and they shake. Edmund forces a smile.

"Take your place over here; we'll get to start the ceremony in a minute." The priest directs Edmund off to his left and nods at the organist, who rises to play.

Her fingers stroke the ivory keys softly, bellowing out a melodic rendition of *The Bridal March*. Anna can feel each note reverberate into her chest, as she makes her way out of the small room at the back of the church, the dangers forgotten. The guests shuffle around to see the elegant Anna coming up the aisle, taking small strides in step with the music, holding her bouquet in front of her waist. Taking the moment in, Anna basks in the glow of her family and friends as she makes her way towards Edmund, the love of her life, wearing her dream wedding dress, a strapless, lilac color hugging her curves. As he approaches the front of the church; Edmund steps down, grasping her hands tenderly, in a loving embrace

The priest steps down, approaching the couple; his bowler hat is still affixed tightly to his head. Edmund looks at him and then up at the hat before turning back onto Anna, concentrating only on the two of them, everything else a starlit blur. Edmund assists her up the small step, holding her hand tightly, locked in each other's gaze, barely hearing the priest.

"Ladies and Gentleman, we are gathered here today to celebrate the culmination of a long relationship, in the joining of two lives into one. Edmund and Anna have asked you here today to celebrate with them in an undying devotion of love, happiness and joy." His words were falling on deaf ears. Edmund and Anna were lost in a world far away from the church, together, seems to them like only mere moments have passed. Those seated in the church heard them recite their vows, appearing to their guests as not missing a beat or being disconnected from the moment.

"Edmund, you may now kiss the bride." Edmund leans slowly into Anna, his lips press firmly into hers. Anna's eyes are closed softly, open to meet his loving stare.

As the priest proclaimed them man and wife, an explosion blew out the church doors, smoke and wood splintering in the air, mildly injuring a few guests. Anna and Edmund grasp each other in a tight embrace as the young organist rushes up to the priest's side, staring at the gaping hole in the side of church, as the guests run screaming from the room. A voice echoes into the church.

"I object to this unholy union." Ambrose James strolls into the church, his flintlock pistol locked and loaded. Three men in all black suits march in behind him, grenades strapped to bandoliers on their chests, and automatic rifles drawn at the ready, locked on the four at the front of the church.

Edmund shields Anna with his body, blocking her from sight. The priest tossed his bowler hat into the air as twelve silver bullets fly up. Edmund and

Anna watch as Jensen sheds the priest color and shirt, just as the organ player tosses him a worn black trench coat.

"RUN!" he shouts, drawing his revolver. The organ player rips her hair tie, releasing her hair and pulls off her Sunday dress revealing tight brown leather pants and black shirt, grabbing her guns from her over the shoulder pistol holder, aiming them at Ambrose.

As gunfire erupts from Ambrose and his cronies, Edmund and Anna sprint towards the nearest side exit, Jensen moves methodically, slapping his revolver's chamber into a seemingly perpetual spin. Olivia's finger pulls smooth and firm on her pistols, the orange fire glistens against the chrome plated firearms. The fog of battle settles into the church. The wooden pews become casualties, sending chunks of wood flying in every direction as they get struck by bullets from the front and rear of the church. Jensen spins as six of the silver bullets track themselves into his violently spinning revolver's chamber. He pulls the trigger. The fire erupts, projecting the first silver bullet rapidly towards the rear of the church. Olivia's blind firing gradually backs Ambrose and his goons out of the church, Jensen's silver bullet buries itself in the leg of one of the grenade toting henchmen. Olivia glances at the side exit to ensure Edmund and Anna have made an escape.

"Jensen, we have to go!" He glances at Olivia, whose eyes burn making her red eyes redder. They slide towards the nearest exit, Olivia slapping the pistols into the holder. Jensen tosses his trench coat around her as they two hastily scurry for the door. The henchmen fire wildly at the trench coat clearly striking it from their point of view.

Firing and reloading as fast as he can, Ambrose rushes toward the side exit. His henchmen, a step behind, unloaded entire magazines through their rifles toward the side exit. All four men stop where the bodies of Jensen and Olivia should have been. Instead at Ambrose's feet are the hundreds of rounds that should have killed Jensen in his stride. The bullets are flattened, almost coin like in appearance, as if they hit something with more force than the firearms could muster.

Ambrose kicks the round, flat objects away and rushes out the side exit. The three henchmen hesitate before sprinting out after him. Ambrose drops his gun to the ground. He looks around at the country hillside. No guests, no Anna, no Edmund, and more troubling, no sign of Jensen and Olivia, just a scenic view of the lush green rolling hills of the remote country setting where the small church sat atop a small hill at the end of the dusty dirt road.

Chapter 16

Edmund's long, labored strides take him away from the Apache prison, his parched throat begging him to stop for air. *"I've got to get back. I've got to find Anna. I need a plan."* His mind churns with thoughts of Anna, as he continually looks over his shoulders to ensure no one is following.

An arid breeze picks up from behind easing his strides and helping to propel his body forward. The breeze gently tugs at his shirt, lifting it up gently off his sweat soaked back, cooling him. He looks one last time, the prison walls blending in with the light sandy dust now spanning back to the horizon. He slows to a quick walk as he crests over a small hill. The city of Apache beacons in the distance. Small lights dot the outlining shadows of the tall skyscrapers that stretch far above the smaller shadows of houses with lights emanating through their windows, occasionally the shadows of the occupants catching Edmund's eyes. He trudges along, his breath slowly returning to him. With each step, the city of Apache gradually grows, engulfing him in its dimly lit night. Edmund moves at a steady pace heading straight towards an old familiar place on an old familiar street.

A rusted out hatchback sits on four flat and bald tires. The naked steel belts glint as Edmund looks the car over, losing himself in his memories. Edmund marched into the old house he once shared with his long lost friend. His recent encounter with his brother had all but confirmed his suspicions that his friend was making a power play to control the

144

town of Apache and to keep time travel under the direct control and influence of Wayne Clayton and Latentech. Edmund flopped on the worn leather couch propping his feet onto a coffee table, flipping the dial on the television. Miraculously the set buzzes to life, electricity still being pumped into the decrepit house, years have passed. He relaxes into the couch.

"One station, all this technology and one station with nothing but Latentech inspired news." He mumbled. *"Breaking News,"* the television blares as Edmund leans forward.

"Ladies and Gentlemen, this is Herbert Golden Walker with a breaking news story here in Apache. Long standing Apache Mayor, Deborah Filmore, has resigned. I say again, Deborah Filmore has resigned. Mayor Filmore had been facing allegations of corruption from Mr. Wayne Clayton of Latentech in an attempt to stop scientific research in Apache. Apparently, Mr. Clayton has provided proof to the Attorney General that the Mayor has been collecting bribes from anti-science supporters. This is in direct violation of the mayoral oath. Furthermore, Mr. Clayton has announced his support behind a new candidate for the mayoral runoff. Ambrose James, lead scientist at Latentech from the Time Research Department. This is a shocking development in Apache. There isn't anyone who has plans or the funding to run against Ambrose James and Mr. Clayton. Outspoken political factions including The Awakened have expressed interest in funding a candidate, but none have come forward. Once again, this is Herbert

145

Golden Walker reporting live from Apache City Hall. A massive power play has occurred and it appears Ambrose James will be an unfettered candidate in the mayoral runoff next week. We now return you back to regularly scheduled programming."

Edmund flipped the remote power button and the Latentech News disappeared from the screen. As he rises from the couch hears a slight clank coming from the kitchen. He looks over to his left, trying to peer through the doorway but it's hard to see into the dimly lit kitchen. He rises, cautiously taking steps towards the doorway. The silent clank repeats, prompting Edmund to freeze.

"Shh, keep it quiet Olivia. I heard him come back. We aren't ready yet." Edmund perks up.

"Olivia," Edmund questions towards the doorway.

Olivia walks through the door and is immediately embraced by her father. He looks over her shoulder, as Jensen exits the kitchen and leans up against the doorframe.

"What, how?" Edmund rattles off questions, causing Jensen smile widely. Olivia pulls back, crying kissing her father on the cheek. Jensen steps forward putting his arm around her shoulders.

"Sit down Edmund; we have a lot to talk about." Jensen guides Olivia around her father and to the couch, the two youngsters plop down, reclining uncomfortably. Edmund follows, sitting on the coffee table in front of them.

"The last time I saw you two was when Anna and I were being arrested. You took off running.

What happened? Where did you run to?" He reaches out to grab his daughter's hand.

Jensen taps Edmund on the knee.

"Remember those pills you said would help us travel through time? Well, we've been a lot of places in a short amount of time. We have to help you come up with a plan to stop Ambrose. The plan has to be rather involved and it may not work out for quite some time, but the future of Apache depends on us coming up with a plan to stop him." He leans back, letting Edmund absorb this information. Edmund shifts uneasily on the coffee table, curious to learn more.

"Tell me what it's like in the future. What does Ambrose do? I just saw on the news he's running unopposed for the next mayoral race. Does that have anything to do with it? What is happening there in the future?" Anxiously, he watches the face of his daughter.

"It's bad Edmund." Olivia began. "Once Ambrose gets elected, he will form the Department of Time Justice. This department will basically control all time travel in Apache as well as be the main law enforcement agency. They will abuse and violate the rights of citizens all over the city. Ambrose will rule with an iron fist. The people will love him at first and then they will fear him. Anyone who stands in his way will be thrown in prison or killed. You, mom, Jensen and I, all end up in prison. This is the future we saw; this is the future that we can't allow." Edmund shifts again on the coffee table, hunching over placing his elbows on his knees and resting his hands on his forehead.

"So, let me get this straight. It's you two and me, up against what sounds like a growing empire of time travelling bad guys who are going to rule Apache because they have nearly unlimited funding and support from a corrupt corporation and CEO, and if we don't do anything our lives are pretty much over as we know it and we have no futures?" His gaze shoots over to Jensen who breaks into a wry smile.

"I've got a plan Ed. Don't worry." Jensen hops up off the couch walking veraciously around the coffee table.

"Listen up, lady and gent. I'm going to let you know how we're going to beat my father. The first thing we must do is make sure he wins the mayoral race. This will allow him to fully entrust Hector, your evil twin brother, to conduct his operations to weed us out. While Hector chases us in this time, we will lure him to the prison where you two, will, in effect switch places. Edmund becomes Hector and Hector becomes Edmund. Olivia will stay at the prison with Anna while you and I, Edmund, put on the largest ruse the City of Apache will never know. You will chase me throughout a decade, allowing me, and maybe at times helping me, to escape the best the Department of Time Justice has to offer. That is going to be the hardest part, if Ambrose even slightly detects that there has been a switch, there will be a force after us so relentless that we might as well commit suicide, because that's what this plan and mission will become. Sounds easy right?" He pats Edmund on the shoulders, chuckling.

"Yeah, easy, you just made the world's largest understatement. Why can't anyone run against him? We know, or I know, more than enough people where we could change the outcome of the election and Ambrose will never get into power." Edmund inquires, facing Jensen.

Rising off the couch, Olivia answered her father.

"See, Jensen believes that Ambrose is letting Wayne Clayton and his materialistic greed influences his process. If he felt like we could knock Ambrose out of that group without the influence of Mr. Clayton and his funding cronies, we would. However, Mr. Clayton and Latentech make billions of dollars a year and we know that a lot of their funding comes from defense systems, plus not knowing how much time travel technology they have developed with the help of Ambrose, puts us at a significant disadvantage. The way we figure is that Mom, Anna, and I can keep the real Hector under control and since Jensen can travel through time with the help of those rift pills easily, all you have to do is maintain Ambrose's trust of Hector. This allows us an inside track to the latest advancements they are making in time travel which keeps Jensen and you, one step ahead at all times." Olivia claps her hands gleefully. Edmund stands, gently scratches his bristly chin.

"How do we start?" He asked concernedly.

Jensen rushes into the kitchen and returns, haphazardly carrying two boxes. He slams them down onto the coffee table. Olivia, giddy with excitement, raises her eyebrows at her father. Jensen opens the top box and removes some clothing, handing them to Edmund.

"For you, we have what will be the Department of Time Justice official uniform, made solely around the chiseled physique of your brother, Hector." Jensen tosses the box to the side and opens the bottom box.

"For me we have something that I procured from a good friend of mine at Latentech." Jensen removes a gloss black trench coat. Edmund stares at it for a moment.

"That's it. You just told me that we have this elaborate plan for controlling the future in Apache and you have a trench coat? You couldn't get any weapons? Or anything that would greatly improve our chances to defeat the massive funding capabilities of Mr. Clayton?" Edmund chastises Jensen, tossing the uniform onto the couch. Jensen smiles,

"Edmund, did I mention I've been to the future? This lame ass trench coat, that I now call my own, is the latest in futuristic bullet shielding technology. Olivia and I have seen what this can do. It will literally stop any bullet from hitting whoever wears it. The bullets smash into it and exert such a force that they flatten on impact. It's pretty cool; you end up with little coin looking remnants from the bullets." Jensen tosses the coat on, quickly fastening the buttons down the front. Olivia looks at Jensen approvingly and then over at Edmund.

"We will do anything to keep us all safe. This is the only way we know how. We know where Mom is. She and I will be safe while you and Jensen do whatever you have to stop Ambrose." She places her hands on her father's shoulders. "You have to trust us, trust what we've seen. Our future, our family, everything is going to fall onto Jensen in the future. If we don't get the upper hand now, our fate is sealed. We have to trust this plan." She hugs Edmund tightly. He looks down at his daughter, willing himself to trust completely in the plan.

"How do we start?" He turns to Jensen and the three kneel down around the coffee table as Jensen details the plan

Chapter 17

Three shadowy figures sprint across the dark landscape of the city, kicking up dust as they move across an arid landscape. The faint dust draws opaque against the stars dotting the night sky before floating harmlessly down to back to the ground. Their strides are long and muffled, as they avoid the main road out of the city, guided only by the stars glimmering across the moonlit eve.

The lead figure comes to a stop a few paces ahead. They sprint up next to the other and they stand quietly, laboring to silently catch their breath. The shadows exchange looks amongst each other as they stare at the towering walls that sit a hundred feet or so ahead.

"The Apache prison gentleman. The first critical part of our plan to stop Ambrose James and Wayne Clayton from destroying everything we know and love." Olivia whispers to Edmund and Jensen, as they begin to discuss their first move.

"The last time I saw Hector was here, this is where I met him and the two members of The Awakened. Gus took me to the cafeteria and then there was gunfire from the interrogation room. That's when he told me I had to run. So I did, as I was running, there was more gunfire. I'm hoping Gus got the upper hand on Hector but, I know my brother. I know he may be in there still. So we will need to be extra cautious. Do you have any ideas of how we're going to get into the prison? The door I ran out of only opens from the inside and we definitely can't just walk up there and ask to be let in." Edmund turns toward Jensen, surveying the distant prison.

While they watch, the massive doors to the prison open slowly with a bright light sneaking out, illuminating the lone road that in front of it. Two figures emerge, illuminated by the light. They look around briefly, donned in protective gear and smaller automatic weapons slung over their shoulders. They lit up cigarettes, the burning embers glowing intensely enough for the trio to see. After a moment, the guards turn back into the light; their intensely burning smokes disappearing with them.

"Well, I guess we know how two of us are going to get in." Jensen turns, Olivia's red eyes glowing slightly in darkness.

Jensen and Edmund move silently against the walls of the prison, while Olivia watches from a distance. Jensen slides quietly, his back pressed against the rough stucco texture of the prison wall. Edmund walks close behind him, crouched down by Jensen's hip, moving rapidly in silence. A faint whistle in the distance reaches the two men, freezing them. Loud thuds shake the sides of the wall forcing Jensen to lean away. Edmund slides away as metal clicks reverberate through the prison walls. Jensen crouches, shuffling to the other side of Edmund as a small crease of light begins to grow a few feet in front of them. Screeching metal rubs together as one of the massive prison door opens. The light from inside the prison grows as the door opens. Two shadows appear, walking towards the open door to grab a smoke. Jensen and Edmund silently watch the men cross the threshold.

The two guards stood mere inches from Edmund and Jensen while they smoked and talked. The guards had brand new uniforms, gloss black from the head to toe, wrapped in thick Kevlar pads at the knees, elbows and chest. The firearms were still shiny, the magazines held tightly in place. It was clear that money has been pumping into the prison from unknown sources. One of the guards slid his hand into his drop cargo pocket to remove a small black container, revealing neatly packed cigarettes. He shakes the container firmly once, two white wrapped smokes slide neatly into his hand.

"Light me up brother, another boring ass night here in lame land." He holds one out for his comrade who takes it quickly while sliding a lighter out from a pocket on his Kevlar chest pad. The two men light their cigarettes and return the container and lighter to their respective places. They stand, leaning their weight heavily on opposite legs. Their chatter is muffled to the two men perched silently behind them.

Edmund nudges Jensen and the two men lunge forward, grabbing the two guards and dragging them into night. The guards gurgle, trying to shout out to their coworkers inside the prison. Jensen and Edmund keep their hands over the mouths and their arms wrapped around their necks. The arms wrapped around their necks tighten as the guards struggle, hoping to be released from their inevitable asphyxiation. Eventually, the guards are still. Jensen turns the neck of his hostage rapidly, feeling a loud click from the guard's neck against his forearm, and the body, lifeless against his torso. Edmund releases his arm from around the other guard's neck, grabbing either side of his head in his hands and twisting rapidly with great force, a loud snap, followed by the slumping body. The two heroes stand and silently drag the men away from the prison, back towards Olivia.

Olivia turns as Jensen and Edmund quickly remove the guard uniforms from the corpses. Edmund slides easily into one set of the black uniforms.

"Well, it still smells fresh, that's always a positive. Feels kind of good to be wearing a uniform, is this what all the hype is about?" He turns, forgetting the uniforms can't be seen in the pitch black. Jensen finishes, struggling with removing the uniform from his guard.

"Olivia, is Anna still in the same cell she was in when you read the scanned files on Ambrose's computer in the future?" He looks at the red eyes that are tracing his figure as he changes.

"As far as I know, I couldn't tell if the prisoner files had been changed or updated anytime recently or in the past. The main thing you need to worry about is Hector. We know he should still be inside based off our research but we don't know who is on his side, so the resistance you face may be massive or it may not be. I would recommend making your way into the cafeteria and look for Gus. He will be able to help, if he is still alive, there is no telling what has happened inside the prison. Judging by the brand new weapons and uniforms, I would suspect you two are in for an uphill battle. Step one, immobilize Hector. Step two, clear the prison. Step three, we secure Anna and begin the first part of our plan." Olivia replies giddily, bouncing on the heels of her feet. She smacks Jensen on the butt as he is shuffling pulling the black guard pants to his waist.

"Woo hoo; I'm totally your fan club president Jensen." She puts her arm around him. "Keep him safe and you know; you should be a little careful too." Jensen winks at her, unseen in the dark. He walks towards Edmund, adjusting his newly donned gear. The two men sling the new automatic rifles into their hands, grasping them firmly.

"Well Edmund, he's your brother. I think it's best you lead the way, you know brotherly love and, well you've been to this prison before." Jensen pats him on his back. Edmund shuffles across the soft dirt with Jensen two paces off of Edmund's right flank. Edmund slides to a stop on the right side of the open door.

Edmund exhales, rushing around the door with Jensen. The center courtyard of the prison is brightly illuminated; the two advance quickly across the open area. The massive metal door that had screeched open shuts rapidly, the metal on metal echoing in the emptiness. Static crackles over a loudspeaker.

"I would stop right there Edmund. You would not believe the pretty young thing I found safely tucked away in this very prison you just escaped from." Edmund pauses, Jensen alongside him, surveying the courtyard.

"Say hello Anna, your husband is here to say goodbye." The voice pierces Edmund's heart, as he drops to one knee in pain.

"Anna." He chokes out her name. Jensen keeps his rifle level spinning slowly, trying to view anyone who may be camouflaged by the now blinding interior lights of the prison.

"It appears you underestimated your brother and his very powerful friends. Now look at you, sniveling on one knee, while some unknown stands more at the ready to face his death than you. Pathetic! To think we came from the same family is appalling. How about you make this easy for me? Drop your weapons and come to the cafeteria. I have the beautiful blushing bride just sitting here, waiting to see you one last time. Then, she will get to watch you die. None of my men will attack you on the way here; just lay down your weapons." Edmund angrily tosses his rifle, heart tight in his chest, looking in the direction of the speaker. Jensen tosses his rifle, it clanks as it bounces of Edmund's and slides into the dirt. Edmund rises off his knee and turns to Jensen. "I'm so sorry." Edmund drops his head in shame as they walk into the prison.

Olivia removes a small pearl hearing device from inside her left ear.

"Jensen and Edmund are in trouble. I have to do something." She paces, pausing every few strides to look towards the prison. She watches as the bright glow behind the prison walls dims, causing the outline of the massive walls to fade into the night.

"Well, I guess I better do something." She takes off through the night until she gets to the prison walls, moving around the entire perimeter, searching for a way in. She comes across a single rusted metal door on the far side of the prison, tugging at it briefly. Kneeling down, she traces the handle until she finds a small keyhole. She cups her hand over her right eye and winces as she closes her eyelid down tightly. She opens her eyelid, as her red iris slides out falling gently into her cupped hand. The dark void where her iris had once been fills in with a faint mechanical whir with another red iris, matching the left side. She slides her thumb over the middle section of the pupil, making it glow. She carefully slides the device into the keyhole, taking a cautious step back.

Inside the keyhole the little red iris glow brighter, changing different colors before sparking into a flame. The metal inner workings of the lock sweat as a strange, powerful heat radiates against it. The flame sizzles as the drops fall off the mechanical pieces, the intense heat occurring melting away the lock and handle mechanisms. The door moves slightly letting Olivia know her path into the prison is now open. She pulls on the handle gently pushing the door open; cautiously craning her head around the frame into a dark hallway. Unhesitatingly, Olivia moves into the prison.

Solemnly, the two men walk along the flickering hallway. Jensen walks behind Edmund, trusting his friend's directional instincts. Edmund purposely continues down dim hallway after dim hallway, hoping to lose Hector's or his minion's tracking ability. Jensen, detecting the uneasiness of their trek through the prison continues on following his friend, desperate to get the upper hand.

Ducking in a recessed doorway, Olivia narrowly avoids two armed guards parading the hallway. She breathes quietly, keeping her eyes tightly closed. Seconds after the guards pass, she slips back into the hallway, moving cautiously, double checking maps and signs. When she reaches the cafeteria, she ducks down when she hears approaching voices.

"Why didn't you dip off into the darkness Jensen? We'd have better odds of getting out of this alive if you wouldn't have stuck so close. This is your plan? For both of us to walk in here, get shot up, and lose Anna forever?" Edmund chastises as he stops in front of the cafeteria doors. Hoping to get some sort of response from Jensen, Jensen's cold dead gaze pierces right through Edmund.

"Not even a word. This is how it's all going to be then? Well, after you. " Edmund curtsies mockingly as Jensen walks by shaking his head. Jensen pushes both doors wide open and immediately hears the flick of a dozen safeties on rifles as he is locked onto by several guards, wearing the same uniform. Edmund ignoring the prison guards tracing and guiding him and Jensen down the middle of the cafeteria, concentrating only on the tied up figure of his wife in a chair. Anna attempts a smile, but the bruise on cheek bones and dried blood on her, prevent it.

"Anna," Edmund rushes to the center of the cafeteria as Jensen continues his slow, steady walk down between the guards. His suspicious gaze sweeps the cafeteria, taking in the blood splatter on walls and the floor.

"Aww, how sweet, it's like a little family reunion. My brother and sister-in-law, here at last." Hector walks up behind Edmund, places himself between Jensen and Edmund. Edmund's hold on Anna is tight, with his head resting on her shoulder.

Tense, Jensen begins to lose his grip on the situation. With Hector blocking Edmund, Jensen forgets about the dozen of trained guards, clenching his fists, pondering how to gain the upper hand.

Suddenly a cry shrieks out from the far end of the cafeteria.

"Let 'er rip, tater chip." Olivia burst through one of the side cafeteria doors in a full sprint.

The trained guards briefly lose focus on Jensen; as he sprints out of the cafeteria, running through the faint light of the halls. Inside the cafeteria, Olivia collides with Hector as a hail of gunfire erupts. The black trench coat unfolds out of her hands and shields Edmund, Anna, Hector and Olivia from the constant barrage of bullets. Hundreds of bullets are flattened and turned into coin shaped remnants as they bounce off the coat and onto the ground. Edmund grabs Hector and the chair Anna is still tied to and drags them toward the side of the cafeteria as Olivia shields them from the onslaught.

The quartet makes it to the side of the cafeteria, attempting to push through the sealed-off side doors. Hector struggles to free himself from Edmund, throwing punches wildly at this brother. Edmund drops Anna and her chair, turning and throwing a single blow to the side of Hector's temple. Hector's eyes roll back as he falls unconscious to the floor. Huddled under the trench

160

coat, protecting Hector, the trio comes under an intense barrage of gunfire. The guards advance, the clanking of empty magazines bouncing off the ground drowns out amidst the loud popping and clinking of bullets flattening as they strike the coat.

Olivia begins to shake, her fear of death overcoming her, losing her grip on the trench coat. The coat begins to fall slightly as rapid gunfire erupts from the opposite side of the cafeteria. Jensen charges in, surprising the guards, he advances on them, his rifle held tightly, fires rapidly, each eruption of the bullet from the muzzle flashing fiery exhaust and light smoke,

The door behind the guards flies open, revealing the massive frame of Gus. He rams into the rear guards using his massive frame to knock them over. He grabs two guards by their helmets, one in each hand and smashes them together. Fresh red blood, mixed with pinkish fluid and chunks of salmon colored matter spew out over his dark hands. Brimming with rage, Gus barrels forward; smashing down onto anyone in his path, with his massive, tree like chiseled legs. As he passes stunned guards, he drives his feet through skull after skull cracking sternum after sternum. Those on the receiving end of his rage; gargle on their own blood. Gus trudges through the bodies, pool of blood and brain matter of the guards, keeping a wary eye on Jensen's advancement, making sure he doesn't catch an inadvertent bullet.

Jensen continues strafing across the front line. Peripherally, he watched as Gus demolished and eradicate a sizable amount of those guards, who were now trying to mount a defensive stance. Jensen's bullets strike through countless limbs, sending flesh and blood cascading across the cafeteria. Managing to maneuver a few feet by Olivia, he kneels down over her parents and Hector. His hands sweat around the grips of the rifle, from his position he can deliver single rounds to the remaining guards attempting to flee from the brutality. Jensen watches Gus as he grabs one of the fleeing guards and lifts him by the neck with one hand. Gus slams the guard down and follows it up with a thunderous stomp of his massive right leg. The crack of a helmet and skull override the faint gargles and moans of dying guards in the cafeteria. Pieces of helmet overrun with blood and pieces of brain matter slide off to the ground as Gus lifts his legs to move towards Jensen.

Gus opens his mouth to say something when the pop of a gun breaks the momentary silence. A single bullet travels through the cafeteria through Gus's massive back and exits with pieces of his heart through a pin sized hole in his chest. Jensen raises his rifle and fires quickly, dropping the already wounded guard. Gus drops to his knees.

"Shit." He falls forward, the blood pooling quickly around him. Jensen looks down at the fallen beast for only a moment, and then turns to Olivia.

"Olivia, it is safe now." He takes the few steps over towards the huddled group; grabbing Olivia's hand which barely has any of the coat fabric in it. The coat falls as she turns on her knees to see Jensen's subtle gray eyes gazing down like halos. Olivia stands, quickly embracing Jensen. Edmund fusses with Anna's restraints freeing her. He hoists her up letting her lean on him, as they survey the cafeteria.

"Well, that was not exactly the plan I had I thought of." Jensen said, breaking the silence. "Well, what's next?" They turn to look down on Hector who seems to be dreaming, a smile on his face. Anna kicks Hector firmly in the back, then spits at him. Edmund wraps his arms tightly around her.

"Now, we get him locked up, get the prison cleaned out, and get ready for the real fight." Jensen turns toward the dozens of bodies; an archipelago of death, islands in the sea of blood.

Chapter 18

A damp, musky smell reaches his nostrils forcing him to wake. He opens his eyes in darkness, blinking several times. He slowly and painfully rises off the cold, damp concrete floor. Jensen desperately feels for something to grab onto, his knees buckling slightly as he gathers himself.

"Olivia? Where are you?" he cautiously shuffles forward. His hand caresses a damp wall, hesitating and then leans against the unfamiliar wall. His eyes grasp for any light source to highlight the surrounding environment. The wet concrete aids the smooth shuffle of Jensen's feet as he struggles to find his way around.

"J-J-Jensen, is that you?" A tender familiar female voice carries through the mysterious black surround. Olivia pushes herself slowly off the concrete; letting out agonizing moans of pain, feeling the effects of the time rift the two young teens had just experienced.

"Yeah, I'm here, keep making noise and I'll make my way over to you." Jensen kept his hand along the wall and began to shuffle towards where he thought he heard Olivia's voice.

"I'm right here. I am so sore. What the hell was that? Do you know where we are?" Her questions guide him along the wall where she now sits on her knees.

"I don't know where we are, or really what happened. The only thing I remember is seeing your sister and then we jumped out to do the time rift. Everything else is really, really hazy. How are you doing?" Jensen reaches out his hand landing on Olivia's shoulder; she jumps and then relaxes as she feels his familiar touch tighten over her. She reaches up placing her hand on his,

"I'm scared Jensen." Her fingers wrap around his, squeezing them lightly.

"I know Olivia, I am too. I think we should try to figure out how to get out of here." Jensen squeezes her hand back. "Come on, I'm close to a wall. I think we can follow it until we can find a light source." He slides his hand into hers grasping it. Olivia places her other hand midway up Jensen's arm and pulls herself to her feet. Jensen shuffles forward, tracing his hand along the wall.

Olivia holds his arm tightly as he leads the way along the dark mass. She can't see anything around them. Occasionally she loses her balance or carelessly brushes the wall with her shoulder. Jensen pauses momentarily at each of Olivia's stumbles to ensure she is alright. She feels his hand tighten around each time; she squeezes back to indicate she is okay. The two crawl along the wall for what seems like an hour before thin light illuminates a door.

"Do you see that? We've found our way out!" Jensen's excited voice carries towards Olivia.

"You, you don't think anything bad could be behind that door do you?" Olivia replied worriedly, squeezing his hands.

"No, I don't think so. You don't have to worry though; you know I'll keep you safe." He squeezes her hands back and walks quickly towards the luminous door frame.

They stand cautiously on each side of the door, patiently listening for signs of danger on the other side. Olivia places her hand carefully against the door. It's cool against her skin and the surface is tacky.

"It's been painted recently, but there is no heat or severe cold conducting against it on the other side. We would be able to feel it on this side. Do you have the handle on your side?" She whispers. "There is a small piece of metal where a handle should be. No handle. We're going to have to pry it open somehow." Olivia hears Jensen's hand slide along the door looking for a place to pry the door.

"I wish there it was lighter, so we could look for a pry bar or pole. Maybe, maybe we should knock?" Jensen chuckles at her simple suggestion.

"Remember, we have people chasing us that shot their way into your house. We don't have guns, and we don't even know how we time rifted in the first place. I think it's too risky." As soon as the words left his mouth, Olivia rapped her knuckles firmly against the door. If there had been enough light, she would have seen the surprised look on his face. They stood, listening for any approaching noise on the other side of the door.

A quiet metallic slide echoes in the darkness. Jensen step away from the door into the darkness. He positions himself dead center of the door so he can grab it as it swings open, so he to duck back into the darkness should this next series of events unfold into a disaster. Olivia slinks behind Jensen off the trapped light struggling to erupt from behind the door. A loud click jostles the door in its frame, loosening from its previous steady state. The rays of natural white light burst into the darkness. A cool rush of air whistles past the door into the damp murky room that is holding them prisoner. The darkness is infused with the brilliant glow of achromatic light. The door swings all the way open catching Jensen off guard. He swipes forward hoping to catch the door but misses. He and Olivia stand face to face with a small child obstructing the path through the doorway.

"Hey, what the fuck are you doing locked in the condemned subway tunnels." The youth spouts boorishly at Jensen and Olivia.

"We got trapped in here somehow, thanks for opening the door for us." Olivia addresses the child.

"Who the fuck would trap someone in here? Were you two fucking in here? I bet you were. Teens are always fucking in the tunnels, better have wrapped your jimmy mate, I bet this fuck gets around on some dicks." Jensen's jaw drops stunned at the little twits vulgarity.

"Excuse me! Where is your mother? You don't speak to people, especially women, like that!" Olivia offended, shouts, vexed at the mysterious child. Jensen strides forward pushing the little, boy, or girl, he can't tell, nor does he really care, to the side. Olivia follows, right on his heels.

"That's right, keep walking, you got caught getting your shit packed in like the dirty whore you are. You're just like all the hookers around here. Go on with you, go finish him off near the boxes like the others do. Dirty fucking sl--," An emphatic smack reverberates off the wall. Olivia draws her hand back shaking it in a veiled attempt to so it again.

"I swear on your mother's fucking grave, if I ever come across you and your putrid language again, I'm going to own your ass. Thanks for opening the door. Now say you're welcome before I toss you out there and leave you to whatever druggies and sex addicts are lurking in the tunnels." Crossing her arms, impatiently, she waits for the youth to apologize. The child looks up at her as its eyes well from the shock of Olivia's hand catching it across the face. A rosy imprint of four fingers begins to swell on its face.

"I'm sorry miss. I was just messing with you." A lone tear rolls down each cheek. Jensen tugs on Olivia.

"Come on, we need to get out of here. Kid, watch your mouth, and thanks again. You never saw us." Jensen and Olivia hurriedly walk down an organized junk of an alley. The youth wiping a tear off its cheek, watches the couple flee with an impish grin on its face.

Jensen and Olivia hastily make their way out of the alley onto a main thoroughfare. Save for a few people a far distance down the street, the walkways and street are void of activity. A brisk gust of wind blows down the street kicking Olivia's black hair up and over her shoulder. Jensen's blonde hair moves gently as grass getting brushed about on an open plain. Their hands interlock as they ponder their next move.

"What shou-," "Where do-," catching one another mid-sentence, they are comforted by the fact that they shared the same concern.

"I guess we need to figure out where we are and what we need to do next." Jensen alludes to the shared thought.

"Yeah, the sooner, the better, I'm ready to get somewhere that feels safe so we can relax, get cleaned up and take inventory on what we know and what we should do next." Olivia places her other hand on Jensen's forearm as she moves closer to him. Jensen looks around gauging which direction to proceed. His eyes catch the bright violet irises of Olivia longingly gazing at him. He winks noticeably pulling her against him and sliding his arm across her shoulders.

"Come on, let's go find out where we are. That will make it easier for us to find a place to stay that we can use to keep a low profile for a day or two." Olivia looks up to him sliding her arm around his back.

"Wherever you go, whatever you do, you know I have to be there now right?" She sees the smile spread across his face.

"Don't get girly on me now Olivia." He brushes her off, attempting to bury his emotions that threaten to bubble up to the surface.

"One day, you'll not be such a badass. I will blackmail the shit out of you when that happens." She buries her head against his chest squeezing Jensen tightly, who reciprocates and pulls her down the path, unaware that they are being watched.

Holding hands, they walk past decrepit apartment buildings and overflowing trash receptacles. Burying her face into his arm, she tries to protect her olfactory senses from the pungent odors emitting from the ramshackle barrio. Jensen pauses and squints into the distance.

"What is it?" She asked in a trembling voice.

"I'm not sure. I'm getting this feeling that someone is watching or following us. It's probably nothing but something doesn't feel right." He looks to either side of him. "Maybe I'm just being paranoid. It's probably just my nerves knowing that someone is following us. Let's get off the street as soon as we can. Apartment or home? I don't have a preference, right now." They quicken their pace, nervously looking for a place to stay, still unaware of that they are being spied on by a child slinking between the shadows, careful not to lets its presence be known.

"You're the ones." The child whispers as Jensen and Olivia walked further away.

At the end of sidewalk, they looked around the unfamiliar ramshackle neighborhood

"Where do you think we can find a place to stay? I kind of like the ambiance." Olivia chuckles; catching Jensen's sigh.

"I don't think we should. We're still much too close to where we came out of the time rift. I would venture to guess people aren't out and aren't going to come out because they know who we are. Or even worse, someone already came here looking for us." A river of asphalt courses through the landscape and beyond the horizon. Olivia tugs on his back, as something clatters on the road behind him. Swallowing his fear, he wraps Olivia protectively in his arms as he chances a glance behind him. The foul mouth child that had assaulted them before lies in a fetal position between a rolling aluminum receptacle and a pile a stacked waste.

"Alright you sadistic little being, why the fuck are you following us?" Olivia demanded, marching up to the huddled, filthy child.

"I, I just wanted to see where you were going, that's all." The child whined, unfurling itself.

"Easy kid, we need to know what the fuck is going on. Where is everybody else? Where are your parents? Something is off about this place and you're going to give us some answers since you took such an interest in our presence here." Jensen drops to one knee placing his hands on the child's shoulders, feeling the bones sticking out through the raggedy clothing.

"What's your name?" He asked, releasing the child.

"My name is Andromeda, daughter of the late Mayor Wayne Clayton. Welcome to Iroquois Jensen James." Olivia gasps as Jensen rises concernedly, stepping back from the girl.

"There is no way that's correct. Wayne Clayton is the head of a very prestigious research company in the city of Apache. Unless there is a severe coincidence in names, I believe you're mistaken." Andromeda jumps, yelling at Olivia.

"I'm telling you the truth! Nobody that comes here ever believes me. Not the vagabonds, not the few left over citizens, and not even the uniformed cops that bring us our monthly rations. Why doesn't anyone believe me?" Shocked by the outburst, Olivia takes a step back; as Jensen places his hand Andromeda's shoulder get her to relax.

"Andromeda, listen. Why were you following us? Did someone tell you to follow us?" Jensen asked gently.

"No. Nobody ever comes to tell me anything. I'm just here. I'm supposed to stay. Wait a second. If you're from Apache how did you get here? You're over three days from there." She asked, piercing Jensen with her stare.

"We don't know how we got here. One minute we were sneaking away from some very bad people and the next minute, we were waking up in those tunnels you let us out of." Olivia crouches down next to Jensen, to Andromeda's level, placing her hands on her knees.

"Andromeda, where is everyone else?"

"Nobody's been here for a while. As far as I can remember, something happened and a lot of people left, some like my dad, died. It wasn't too long after that when we started getting rations." Andromeda's head droops, and then rises quickly. "Are you guys going to stay here?" She asked, shuffling her feet on the sidewalk.

"Funny you should ask that, we're trying to find a place to stay for a couple days. Do you know a place?" Olivia stands a little smiling down at the cute, ratty haired, vulgar brat.

"You can stay with me! Come on! My place is perfect for all of us." Andromeda beamed.

172

"Your guardians or roommates won't mind?" Jensen inquired, still on his knees.

"No, no one will mind. Everyone is gone. I've got my own place. Has the best view of Iroquois and a lot of amenities." Andromeda sped off, pausing to turn around briefly. "Well, come on. It's going to be awesome!" She sped off, with Olivia and Jensen in pursuit.

The remnants of Iroquois pass as Andromeda leads Olivia and Jensen along the main road towards a dull and dusty glass tower building. Andromeda runs through a set of rotating doors, leaving Jensen and Olivia outside. They contemplate the eerie familiarity, wondering if it's their version of Wayne Clayton, back in Apache.

The doors lurch as Olivia walks through, Jensen right behind her. They are greeted by an unpleasant odor.

"Don't mind the smell. There is no power here so the air doesn't circulate. Come on, we're almost there. There are just a few flights to make it to the top." Andromeda pushes open a door a few paces from what looks like an entry way to a lobby of elevators.

"She must not get a lot of visitors." Jensen observes as he pushes the door open for Olivia. Andromeda stops a few flights up to look down at them.

"Come on you two, if we're lucky I can show you some of the city before the darkness comes." Her excitement motivates Jensen and Olivia to follow her.

Slightly winded, they watch Andromeda open the last door, motioning them to hurry with her hand. Pursing Andromeda, Olivia enter the room, stunned. The room was full of lavish furniture, making the ratty appearance of Andromeda seem out of place. Jensen, leery, surveys his surroundings, taking in the dining room table set for three.

"I told you I had a really nice place. It's the nicest place in Iroquois. It came with all this furniture and when the power is on, I have all kinds of cool gadgets." Andromeda runs through the room and flops down on a massive white leather sectional.

Entering the tiny kitchen Jensen discovers piles of canned goods, boxes of crackers packed neat and tight against the backsplash. Jensen imagines what it might be like to prepare a meal in this space, at a different time, like his mother used to do.

"Um, yeah it's all non-perishable. That's what they bring every month. I go out to the pallets and make sure I get enough for every month." Andromeda explained, appearing next to Jensen.

"So, it's just you, on your own? No one else lives here?" Jensen asked.

"Yep, I'm pretty much the Mayor." She smiled emptily.

"Wait. You mean you live in this entire city by yourself? There is no one else?" Finished with her tour of the immense space, Olivia entered the kitchen.

"Except for a few wanderers and vagrants, I'm the only true remaining citizen of Iroquois."

Sitting at the dining room table, Jensen and Olivia wait as Andromeda finishes putting together her plate of food from the cans. As they eat, Jensen and Olivia are amazed that the food is still palatable, remarking on how even the crackers were still crisp.

Satisfied from the meal, Andromeda shuffles around picking up the plates and tosses them down the garbage chute.

"Why did you do that? It was nice." Olivia asked.

"The water is only on the morning. Plus, I have lots of dinnerware." Andromeda giggled. Jensen excused himself from the table to peer out the glass wall that overlooks Iroquois. The sun has begun its gradual decline beyond the horizon. Andromeda and Olivia join him.

"It's beautiful right? I watch it every night. It feels better watching it with people." Andromeda sighed with a tinge of loneliness.

"It's very beautiful Andromeda. One should never have to watch something so beautiful alone." Caught in the moment, Jensen and Olivia place their hand on Andromeda's back, as the sun disappears under the horizon.

"Andromeda, tell us what happened to this place. What happened in Iroquois?" Jensen gently asked, sitting next the little girl on the massive couch, with Olivia on her other side. Hesitantly at first, then building speed with clarity and profanity, she talks about her supposed father, Wayne Clayton, then a secret research project gone awry, causing a mass exodus of the citizens, ending with the death of her father and her abandonment. Exhausted by telling her story Andromeda rests her head against Olivia's arm and quickly falls asleep. "

"What do you think she's going to dream about?" Jensen asked, sliding his arm around Olivia.

"Not being alone anymore." Closing her eyes, Olivia leans her head against Jensen arm and falls asleep. Unable to resist, Jensen closes his eyes, falling asleep to thoughts of family, as darkness engulfs the room.

Chapter 19

The sun beams bright in through the dulled glass wall, revealing Olivia and Andromeda nestled against each other. Jensen awake and in the bathroom, double checks the shower, making sure the water is on. Switching the dial, water trickles out of the shower head, muddied at first, followed by a clear hot stream of pure liquid. The steam rises toward the ceiling. After a quick examination of his body in the mirror, he steps in, letting the soothing warm water cascade over his body. Placing his head against the wall, he inhales the hot steam.

The door creaks, jostling Jensen. "Who's there?" He commands faintly. The curtain opens and Olivia's nude body joins his in the shower, the water turning her hair a glossy jet black. The water spraying off her body is more than Jensen can handle. Her eyes look right into his as her hands grasp his waist, pressing into each other, as they passionately begin to kiss each other, groping each other. Jensen kisses down her neck as he lifts her, pressing her back against the wall. Her legs wrap tautly around his hips as the intimate embrace begins. Olivia gasps as she feels herself fall deeper in love with her childhood friend. Jensen's tender kissing is countered with Olivia's hands clutching his body with intensity. Their lips meet again as their bodies stay entangled in their tangled loving web. Moments later, Olivia shakes and Jensen quivers, then they both sigh and relax. They kiss each other's bodies feverishly, slowly separating from their entanglement.

"We're all we have, Jensen. I've never told you this, but I've always loved you." Her hands run through his hair as they stay locked in each other's gaze. Jensen kisses her deeply again.

"I won't ever leave you. You're my destiny. I've always wanted to be yours. I love you too, Olivia Jima." They finish their shower with intimate kisses and soft touches while they dry.

In the kitchen, Andromeda worriedly opens up a few cans of fruit and another box of the crisp crackers.

"Good morning!" She nearly sings out her greeting, as Jensen and Olivia enter the kitchen, relief flooding her face that her guests had stayed. The trio gathers at the table, consuming the not quite satisfying but filling breakfast of fruit and crackers. After everyone finished, Olivia clears the table, putting off Andromeda weak murmurs of dissent.

"So Andromeda, do we get a tour of Iroquois today?" Jensen asks, wondering how she could have survived on her own for so long. Squirming off her chair, Andromeda ignores the question and goes to the window, staring out. Olivia joins her, sitting on her knees.

"Andromeda, how long have you been living like this? Has no one come to look for you or any other remaining citizens of Iroquois?" Andromeda stares at Olivia, frowning.

"I was seven when everyone left me behind. I'm at least nine now. I think. I'm not sure I've lost track of the days. I lost count. Sometimes, the uniforms, they come looking for people. They don't come into the buildings though. So I stay here. I don't trust them. They're scary." Olivia hugs her tightly.

"Is it safe to go out today? Jensen and I have a lot to figure out about how we got here and what we need to do." Olivia asked placing her hands on Andromeda's arms. Andromeda nods.

"Today is safe. I have some folders that look important that you can look through. I think they're about what happened here. I tried to read them, but I don't understand them. I'll be right back." As Andromeda rushes off of the room, Jensen and Olivia stand to sit on the couch.

A box skids across the stained wood floor, stopping at Jensen and Olivia's feet. Panting, Andromeda plops on the floor in front of them.

"It's kind of heavier than I remember." The blue box is marked with the word Confidential, its lid ripped up, as if tape had sealed the contents. Jensen removes the lid and sifts through the stacks of files and folders. There are dozens of folders containing experiments ranging from time travel to genetic manipulation. Jensen picks up a folder with the name "James" stamped neatly across the tab. He rips it open; discovering an entire personnel file with a picture of a younger Ambrose James in a lab coat and nametag, standing beside Wayne Clayton.

Squinting, Jensen makes out *Lead Researcher* on the tag. Waves of feelings rush over him, hitting him with his mother's death and the mystery of his now disconnected father. Questions and emotions overwhelm him, causing him to drop the folder and stand to get a drink, Andromeda pattering after him. Curious, Olivia picks up the dropped folder.

She gives the file a cursory glance; she sifts through the remaining ones. She picks one that contains information on Iroquois, and a listing of all the citizens in alphabetical order. Initially stunned, she checks for familiar names, but comes up with only Ambrose.

Continuing her search, she discovers Wayne Clayton's name, a woman's name who she surmises is Mrs. Clayton, but curiously enough, there is no sign of Andromeda, even after a thorough examination of the list. Olivia checks the date on the report. It's less than a year old. Worried, Olivia starts to think that something is seriously wrong.

Andromeda follows the path of Jensen's pacing at the far end of the room. Trying to ignore her, he feels himself being pulled in by her innocent and non-judgmental air. He pauses in front of her then sits down next to her.

"You saw something in there that's bad didn't you?" He asked Andromeda, her cheek resting on her hand, eyes staring inquisitively at him. "There are a lot of bad things and people in the world Andromeda. A lot of them that I have come in contact with are in that little box of files you brought to show me." Andromeda scoots closer crossing her legs and putting her elbows on top, her chin squishes down into her hands, a faraway look in her eyes. He rustles his hand through her hair making her giggle slightly. Her smile quickly fades.

"Andromeda, what's troubling you? Where and how did you get that box?" Jensen asked.

"Hurmph!" She spins around on the floor, turning her back on him.

"Andromeda, Olivia and I need all the information we can get. If we can keep each other safe, then with all the knowledge of what happened here, we can keep you safe." Jensen slides around on the floor positioning himself in front of the disconnected little girl. "It's not just your file that's in there. My file is in there too. Everything you need to know is in there." A single tear escapes and rolls down her cheek. Jensen stands and looks over towards Olivia who's still scanning through the box. He looks back down at Andromeda.

"Come on. Let's go look together. You'll be able to tell me all about what you know that's in your file. I'll be able to tell you all about Ambrose. Then Olivia and I can tell you all about what we know and how we got here. Sound fair." He extends his hand down for Andromeda, who grabs it, pulling herself off the floor. The two walk back and take seats on either side of Olivia.

Olivia has a few files set out spread out in front of her, entranced in one of the files, barely noticing as Jensen and Andromeda sit beside her. Finishing she turns to the both of them.

"Andromeda and I have an agreement to tell each other everything we know. Sound interesting?" He asked, sliding his arm around Olivia, laying her head against his shoulder.

"You go first Andromeda. Nothing but the truth, I've looked through the folders." Olivia speaks authoritatively. Andromeda sighs and nervously picks at her nails, her long ratted hair hiding her face.

"My name is Andromeda. I do not know my last name and I never met Mr. Clayton. I was a wanderer with a family, who left me here. I thought of Mr. Clayton as a father because his company funded my orphanage here in Iroquois. I was left behind after I was caught looking for food inside the main company building, where I live. I don't remember a lot, but when they kicked me out of the orphanage is when I started stealing supplies and those files. Then one day, I woke up and found everybody gone. It was like they all moved away while I was asleep. I was scared. I have lived on my own since then. Sometimes wanderers come by and I have to chase them away because I like being here. I feel safe on my own, because nobody will live alone if no one is here to keep me company. I found files about Ambrose and time travel, I knew Jensen existed from his dad's biography, but I didn't recognize you at first. I shouldn't have lied to you, but I shouldn't have let you come here. The uniforms always talk about looking for someone. I think that's you." Andromeda, teary eyed looks up from her curtain of hair.

As Olivia pulls her in for a hug, she explains about their lives back home, about Maria, Jensen's family, the Jima's, everything she remembered. Andromeda peered around Olivia to look at Jensen.

"I'm sorry about your mom. Do you miss her?" Jensen sits up, peering down in her innocent eyes.

"I do. Just like Olivia misses her family. One day, I hope to get the people who took our families

182

from us and put them away so they stop doing bad things to others." He explained.

"You know, we're kind of like a family now. I don't have a family, at least, not that I know of. I feel safe with you and her here."

"You're tired of feeling lonely too huh?" Olivia asked squeezing her a little tighter. Andromeda emphatically nodded her head. After a moment of comfortable silence, Jensen stands.

"I'd still like to take a tour Madam Mayor." Andromeda rushes to the door, jumping up and down like an excited puppy. Olivia and Jensen follow the excited youngster as she makes a beeline down the stairs and into the lobby of the building.

Chapter 20

Emerging from the rotating glass doors, Andromeda hurries out into the city of Iroquois, Jensen and Olivia maintaining a comfortable stride behind her.

Compared to Apache, they notice that there isn't much to Iroquois. It has the main street, surrounded by a slew of residential buildings. The old research building, which now serves as Andromeda's lavish skyline apartment, stands as the focal point to the small town. A few alleyways are scattered about the row of residential buildings. A small handful of storefronts also dot the main street. There were no signs or remnants of a larger city.

As she gives them a tour, Andromeda talked about the days leading up to when everybody left, what she was doing and where she was, and describing some individuals in details, others as shadows on the street, wondering aloud if she would have liked any of them.

The walk which was supposed to be a simple way of getting to know the city had turned into a game with Andromeda constantly running through alleyways, checking for things to take. Jensen makes a better show of hiding his frustration while Olivia's frustration is visible across her face.

"Andromeda, come on now! We just need to finish looking over what around Iroquois and then you can play around." Olivia angrily shouts at the little girl, growing impatient with her incessant dawdling. Andromeda's shoulders droop as she kicks her feet at the ground, irritated at having to be told what to do, by adults. She drags her feet over to Olivia and Jensen, pouting and crossing her arms. Jensen chuckles and begins to walk back to the large glass building in the distance, with Olivia and Andromeda following.

"I don't think there is much else for us to see right? Not really a big enough city to stay safe in. I think we need to get back and start planning our trip to Apache. I think that's where we need to go to find answers." Jensen slows so Olivia could wrap her hand in his as Andromeda skips on by, leading the couple back to her living space. A calm which they had not felt since being passionate intertwined falls over them as Olivia kisses him tenderly on his cheek.

As they entered the neglected building, it seemed like decades since the building was the center of a bustling, growing city. Jensen and Olivia reflect on how Andromeda could have survived the mass departure of the citizens of Iroquois, leaving nothing behind but trash and the decaying city.

"Why are you guys always staring at me?" She asks, somersaulting in front of them.

"Well Andromeda, it's kind of a remarkable thing for you to have survived so long on your own. You're obviously a very smart little girl." Andromeda beams, half curtseying at the compliment.

As Jensen rises off the couch, he kisses Olivia on the forehead. Olivia reflects on their predicament, calm that Jensen is there, knowing that she should be more afraid. Curiously, she wonders if he is more cautious of his surroundings because of her. As her eyes trail his movements from the room, she notices that Andromeda is watching her watch Jensen.

"And why are you looking at me like that?" She asked the blushing little girl.

"I think it's cute that you two are in love. I bet that makes what you're going through easier." Andromeda observes, snuggling next to Olivia.

"Well, I guess we make it a little obvious don't we?" Putting her arm around Andromeda the little girl watched as a quick iridescent red flash replaced the violet in one eye before it reverted back to Olivia's original color. Andromeda tilts her head curiously.

"Your eyes are funny." Andromeda's hand rubs Olivia's cheek, pointing towards the center of the violet iris.

"Why do you say that little one?" Olivia asked.

"I just saw them change colors and then back again. It was weird." Andromeda, thought clenched her fingers into a fist, bringing them to her lap. Olivia paused.

"Well, you probably just think you saw them change. My eyes have always been violet, they don't change." She explained.

"Oh, okay." Andromeda hops off the couch, pulling Olivia up with her, and they start dancing around in the remaining light streaming through the dull and dirty window, Andromeda pretending to catch it in her hand.

As they dance, she keeps catching the quick iridescent flashes of red, replacing the violet iris in Olivia's eye. Fascinated, she slows her movements, catching more and more of the red light in her eyes. Olivia, noticing that her dance partner has stopped, crouches down as a deep glow fills in her iris before disappearing.

"What's the matter Andromeda?" Olivia asked, holding her hand.

"Oh, I don't know. You're just really pretty." Andromeda beams brightly again, her little fingers squeeze Olivia's hand.

"Andromeda, are you going to go with us when we leave?" Olivia stands, watching as Andromeda struggles for an answer.

"I think I want to go. I'm tired of being here. There are no people and I get really bored."

"Well, you should come with us. Apache is a really nice place. Plus, we will be safer there while we search out answers to our predicament. There would be a lot of children your age for you to play with." Olivia offers. Andromeda gives Olivia a half smile, as she wanders to the other side of the apartment to think over the offer.

Jensen stands above the box of files on a bed that looks like it hasn't been slept in since it was made. His eyes are locked onto the images of his father and Wayne Clayton. Questions and concerns fill his mind about what lies in store for the Jima's and his and Olivia's future in Apache. His thoughts wander to the subject of Andromeda and how she could have survived for so long and debates on whether to take her with them. Running his fingers through his hair continues sifting through the box.

He stumbles across a picture of a young girl, maybe two or three years old. He flips it over and written in perfect cursive penmanship is the name *Andromeda James Clayton*. Sliding it into his pocket, he continues rifling through the remaining files. Nothing strikes his interest until he finds a folded piece of paper tucked neatly under the seam of the box. He slides it out opening it carefully to read the sloppily written text.

Don't let the girl die. The red eyes are everywhere. The red eyes are

The handwriting seems familiar but Jensen is unable to place it. He refolds the paper and slides it in next to the picture of the young girl in his pocket.

"What are you doing Jensen?" Jensen jumps and turns to see Andromeda in the room.

"Oh nothing was just scanning through these files again, hoping I could have found something that would have helped us out when we go to Apache." He smiles, putting the files back in the box. Andromeda nods, then abruptly turns around and leaves Jensen standing in the room by himself. *What an odd little girl* he shakes this thought off and sets the box back on the bed. His stomach growls as he makes his way to the kitchen.

Entering the kitchen, he greets Olivia with a soft kiss. They stand next to each other, their fingers intertwined.

"So, have you thought about what we should do about Andromeda? I already asked her if she wanted to go with us to Apache and she seems a little interested. I really think she wouldn't be too big of a burden for us. She is pretty much self-sufficient and I don't think she would slow us

188

down." Olivia breathlessly rushed out. Jensen ran his fingers through his hair, answering her slowly.

"She has to come with us. I'm not sure why, but I think she's important to everything with this time travel stuff. As much as I think she would be fine here on her own, and that she might put us in more danger somehow. She has to go with us."

"Why do you feel that way?" Olivia's warm hand comforts Jensen.

"I'll tell you everything once we get on the way to Apache. I also think the sooner we live the better it will be for all of us." Jensen forces a smile and swoops in kissing Olivia on the cheek. They tightly embrace each other, lost in the moment, not realizing little eyes peered at them from the opposite side of the counter.

"Are you guys' hungry?" Jensen and Olivia unfold from each other and spot Andromeda staring at them over the counter. She shakes her head as she grabs a couple of cans of fruit and the crackers.

"Just think, in a couple days we will be in Apache and you will get to eat anything you want for the first time in years. I know I would be sick and tired of fruits and crackers." Olivia runs her hand through Andromeda's hair. Andromeda grabs the plates and rushes them to the table, sitting first, as Olivia and Jensen take their places.

"Sometimes, I've been thinking, anyways, that I don't want to leave. You and Olivia are really nice though and I like being around you guys. I think that's why I'm going to go, because if you leave then I'll be alone again. I don't want to be alone, because then I'm sad. So, it makes sense that I am going to go with you." Andromeda mashes some fruit onto a cracker, biting into them violently.

The three of them eat, mimicking each other's movements, almost as if they were a real family. At the end, full but not satisfied, Jensen excuses himself and moves towards the bedroom where the box of files still sits on bed. He pulls the box off and sets it on the floor. He tosses his clothes off as he climbs into the sheets, closing he eyes

In the living room, Olivia tucks Andromeda in on the sofa, the little girl's hair flowing gently over the blanket.

"Everything will be great Andromeda. You'll be safe with us." Olivia leans, kissing her softly on the cheek. As Olivia turns to go to her room, Andromeda catches an eerie red glow sneaking out from behind the violet iris.

Shutting the door behind her, Olivia starts shedding her clothes, pausing briefly when she notices Jensen, now wide awake, watching her. Clad only in her bra and marching bikini bottoms, she leans over to kiss Jensen. He pulls her on top of him as they kiss passionately. As he wanders over her body, he firmly grasps her thighs before caressing up her stomach to her firm breasts, gently moving his thumb over her nipples, still tucked away in a lilac brassiere. Their next kiss is deep, their tongues dance and slide across each other. Finding her way out of her undergarments, she slides down under the sheets on top of Jensen. Exploring, she runs her hand runs down his stomach and into his boxers, removing them and gently stroking him. They kiss deeply again, she can feel his gentle lips against her breasts. Olivia grinds her hips against his, embracing him tightly between her legs. He gently rolls her over on to her back. Their sweaty, passionate bodies move in unison, hips snug against each other. Moaning softly, their bodies clench once, before relaxing on top of each other. Jensen rolls off Olivia, kissing her tenderly, as she moves her head on his chest. Interlocking their fingers, Jensen gazes into her vivid violet eyes, as a faint, red flash sprints across her eyes. Jensen blinks, her eyes are the same vivid purple.

"Tomorrow is important." He whispers as she listens to his heartbeat. She rises up kissing Jensen deeply, her firm bosom presses against his chest.

"You have no idea." Her words fall onto deaf ears; Jensen is already asleep. Olivia's smile dissipates as she drifts off to sleep on his chest, preparing for tomorrow.

Chapter 21

Olivia carefully places the small, curved, circular device onto her eye. Her red iris rolls down catching the implant, positioning it perfectly. Looking into the mirror, one deep violet eye and one deep red eye stare back at her. With a heavy heart, her thoughts run back to her family and then to Jensen. She knew that she loved him, but she has a decision to make and a job to do. It wasn't about love, it was about family and stopping Ambrose James the only way she was taught how. She had to be the one to kill Jensen James. She places the second ocular implant over her iris, blinking away the irritation. Admiring her body in the mirror, she starts playing with her long strands of jet black hair thinking of the shared intimacy of last night. Shaking her head to clear it, she dresses and goes to wake him up.

"Wake up lover," she said leaning over to kiss him as he sits up, his blonde hair matted down.

"Morning Olivia," he smiles back, clearing his throat as he sits up. They kiss lightly and smile foolishly. Olivia sets Jensen's clothes on the bed next to him.

"Come on, get ready. We have a long trip ahead of us. I'll go wake up Andromeda and make sure she is ready to go," said Olivia over her shoulder as she left the room.

In the bathroom, Jensen stares soberly at his reflection, thinking how the responsibility of the two girls rests on his shoulder. Pulling his shirt over his head, the sleeves sit taut on his biceps, the rest of the shirt falling loosely over the waistband of his pants. Briefly, he remembers the trench coat Mr. Jima handed him before the rift and if it had managed the trip with him. Panicked, he runs out of the bathroom to search for it, knowing that he misplaced it.

As he searches the room, he glanced at the cracked open door of the closet. Driven by paranoia, he pulls the door open to find the black trench coat hanging neatly, along with a tilted black Stetson on the top shelf. Throwing on the trench coat, he discovers it a perfect fit. He grabs the Stetson and tilts it down over his brow. His hand grasps for the object the Stetson was on, pulling back a black leather gun belt, with two revolvers, with six rounds in the revolving chambers.

At first, he thinks the silver, shimmering rounds are false. Awestruck, he carefully slings the gun belt around his waist securing it tightly. It fits, but droops a little on his left, clearly intended for a larger framed man. He jogs in place, satisfied that it won't fall off. Jensen tosses the trench coat tail up and lets it fall into place, securing only the middle button on his chest. He leaves to find the girls.

Olivia, braiding the little girl's hair by the window, sizes up Jensen as he walks in.

"I always wondered who that outfit was for." Andromeda said, turning back to the scene outside the window. Putting a ribbon at the end of the braid, Olivia nods, also distracted.

"I like it. Seems fitting for what we're about to go through. I think we have a problem though," she said, motioning at the window.

"Those are the uniformed men that usually bring the rations, but something is different." Andromeda pauses. "They look like they're going through and looking for people in the buildings." Looking down, he notices that for each building at least twenty of these armed individuals are entering the building. Fear rises in his throat, as he realizes they have overstayed their welcome in Iroquois. He starts to grab the provisions from the kitchen.

"Grab whatever you can. We have to get out of here fast." Scurrying they grab whatever clothes and additional food they can fit into one backpack, stuffing it until they can see the seams. Hastily, they run out of the apartment and down the stairwell.

Jensen and Olivia quickly run down the stairs, pausing occasionally for Andromeda to catch up to them. In seconds they are in the lobby, and Jensen runs to the front rotating doors. He can see many more uniformed personnel scouring the streets, clearly looking for someone in particular. The fear he felt in the Jima house overwhelms him, knowing that the only hope for Olivia and Andromeda is to create a distraction for them to escape. He paces as he tries to come up with a plan where someone may not end up dead, particularly him. Accounting for all the officers outside the building, he makes his way back to Olivia and Andromeda.

"I have a plan to get you and Andromeda out of here," He said to Olivia, tugging her out of Andromeda's earshot.

"There are these uniformed soldiers or cops, or whatever outside the front and off to the left side of the building. There is an emergency exit on the right rear of the building. I'm going to run out and distract them and you and Andromeda can make a beeline for the back. I'll meet up with you guys somewhere out behind the building, maybe a mile or so." Olivia, shocked stares at him.

"Hey, you have to do this, there isn't another way. We don't know who they are or why they are looking for us. We can't run the risk of them catching us. We don't know their intent." Placing his hands on her shoulders, he can feel her tense up.

Teary eyed, she nods and wraps her arm around his neck, passionately kissing him for what feels like an eternity. Reluctantly breaking their kiss, Jensen walks with Olivia over to Andromeda. He pats her on the head and explains that she is to go with Olivia no matter what.

Nodding, she quickly hugs him around the waist. He gives her one last smile making his way to the rotating doors. Andromeda and Olivia watch Jensen walk out of the rotating doors, they both sink inside. As tears run down Olivia's cheeks, Andromeda reaches for her hand, her little heart hurt. She didn't understand whether she was sad for Olivia or sad for Jensen, but Andromeda could feel something that she didn't like. As Andromeda leads Olivia toward the rear emergency exit door, she feels Olivia pull back on her arm.

"Come on Olivia, we need to go!" Andromeda pulls again to no avail. "Come on Olivia!"

She turns shouting, as she tries to pull her arm away but Olivia's grip tightens around her hand.

"Ouch. Olivia you're hurting me. Stop it! That hurts." Andromeda whimpers as Olivia keeps a firm grip on her hand. With her other hand, she removes the two violet ocular devices that had been masking the iridescent red glow of her true eye color. Ignoring her cries, Olivia drags Andromeda whimpering and struggling towards the front of the crystalline façade.

Two groups of the mysteriously uniformed clad personnel turn towards Jensen as he walks out into the street. As they converge towards him, Jensen begins to feel that perhaps, he won't be rejoining Olivia and Andromeda. Sweating, he slowly backs away as hundreds more uniformed personnel beginning to converge in front of the glass tower building, forming an immense semi-circle around him. Taking a deep breath he places his hands on his waist, falling on the handles of his revolvers. As he touches them, a sense of calmness overwhelms him, knowing he has a secret weapon.

"Nobody else will get hurt if you come with us Jensen. We want you and Andromeda. This can end peacefully," A lone gunman walks up, pausing ten feet from Jensen.

"How do you know who I am?" Jensen drops one hand to his side as the other raises to the middle button of the trench coat, ready to toss the coat open for him to grab his revolvers.

"You and Andromeda just need to come with us. You're surrounded." Looking around, he notices the hundred or so uniformed personnel; every one of them has a gun drawn with a bead on him. Circling, he comes to a stop at the rotating doors of the glass building.

Olivia stands, holding Andromeda's wrist firmly in her hand, a fiery glow emanating from her eyes. Jensen's heart drops into his stomach and rises into his throat all in one motion.

"Olivia, no, no, what are you doing?" he shouts at her. Smiling impishly, she pushes Andromeda into the waiting arms of a few of the armed guards.

"I love you, but this is about family." Olivia rushes forward, charging him. As he tosses open his trench coat he is tackled by the guard, who holds his arms down as Olivia delivers a solid elbow to his nose, sending blood streaming out of his nostrils. As he struggles to free himself, Olivia swings wildly, catching him in the jaw. Stunned, he is taken aback by Olivia's strength and fighting prowess. Another guard charges at him, but at Jensen dives out of the way Olivia kicks him in the chest, bringing him to his knees as he stumbles to put some distance between himself and his assaulters, as Olivia closes in on him quickly.

Jensen can hear Andromeda's muffled screams. He remembers the revolvers still snug against his hips. As the guard and Olivia catch up to him and swing for him with their fists, he quickly unbuttons the trench coat, ducking as the trench coat falls to the ground in between them.

The guard pauses, looking at the revolvers.

"Well things just got a little more interesting." Jensen dodges the rushing guard, only to catch a punch to his mouth from Olivia. Jensen's eyesight blurs as he struggles to dodge and dive out of the reach of his relentless attackers. As Olivia charges him one more time, Jensen swings his hand down onto one of his revolvers, sliding it effortlessly out of the holster. Gripping the pistol tightly, he swings it into the side of Olivia's jaw. A thud, a crack, followed by a shrill of pain radiates from Olivia. With the guard distracted, Jensen sights the revolver up; smacks the hammer back, and pulls the trigger, causing the revolver chamber glows an incandescent blue, as a silver bullet erupts from the barrel with a crack of smoke and fire. Awestruck, he watches the bullet slice through the guard's chest, dragging the bloodied flesh from his organs and skin behind it. The guard slumps to his knees, then to the ground.

Rising quickly, he tosses on the trench coast as gunfire erupts from the massive semi-circle in front of him. He makes a quick line towards the guards holding Andromeda, lining each one quickly on the iron sight of the revolver, pulling quickly on the trigger. The revolver cracks thunder as the indigo fire burns intensely in the revolving chamber. He quickly grabs her and dives behind a small concrete planter box as the three guards fall. Andromeda tucks her head in against Jensen's chest as fragments of concrete and dust shower down around them. Jensen looks down as Andromeda breathes frantically. He wraps the trench coat over her while frantically checking her for wounds. Crimson liquid stains the shoulder of her white cotton dress. Pressing the area lightly, Andromeda winces in pain. The concentration of gunfire shattering on the concrete grows. Shuddering, she takes a deep breath then lies still against his chest. Everything blurs as a waves of fear and sickness overtake him plunging him into darkness, as he collapses over Andromeda.

The firing stops as a team of five uniformed guards' line up, two on the far side of the planter, the remaining three on the closer corner, directly in front of the rotating doors. The closer team motions to the two on the far side to engage around the corner. They move swiftly with their guns raised, resting on the triggers as they maneuver with tactical precision. They round the turn and immediately lower their firearms. They motion to the other three members of the fire team. All of them stand over the seemingly lifeless body, her blond hair lying in a pool of blood growing beneath her small body. Speak inaudibly, they wave their hands in a motion to the other guards and the semi-circle disburses, turning away from the glass building.

As the uniformed guards disperse, a figure emerges from the rotating glass doors in glass façade of the building. Black boots step into the pool of blood around Andromeda's body, kneeling and scooping her body into its arms. As he picks her up her chest rises and falls heavily, straining for life. Walking away from the pool of blood, the prints disappear three feet from the blood. The mysterious figure and Andromeda disappear without a trace from the city of Iroquois.

Jensen James opens his eyes to a small, strange bedroom, crammed with a large bed and nightstand. The walls are barely noticeable in the black, vacuous night. Jensen rolls over. His body, his face, sore. He brings his hand to his face, touching a dried substance caked around his lips and nostrils. He blinks, the pain is nauseating. He closes his eyes. He exhales "Andromeda" before succumbing to the pain and nausea, drifting into unconsciousness.

Chapter 22

A confused and disoriented Olivia pushes off the concrete slab outside of the decrepit, broken down glass enclosed high rise in Iroquois, wondering what happened to Jensen, Andromeda and the uniformed guards.

I must have time rifted, which means Jensen time rifted. Olivia's returning memory settles her initial shock of her surroundings. She takes inventory of her body, rubbing her hurt jaw and patting off the dust on her leather pants, wondering what her next move would be. She looks back at the dilapidated building where it seemed just hours ago she was ten years younger, turning her back on a young man who had sworn to love and protect her. It was growing painfully obvious that they had both rifted, and Jensen left Olivia to lie unconscious in the ruins of Iroquois. She turns back down the long strip which once housed the high-rises, casinos and storefronts, the ruins resembling a place once on the cusp of cutting edge civilization, as well as the debaucherous nature of humanity. Olivia stretches as she investigates the main street, taking a few minutes to get to the edge of town. In the distance, she can see Apache sprawling across the empty wastelands. The city has grown; the skyline illuminates the horizon with dark shadows of architectural wonder. She kicks a loose rock into the wasteland, watching as a cloud of dust rise and trails behind the meandering sediment. She begins her long walk back to the Apache city limits.

Olivia's clothes stick to her back as she makes her journey through the badlands separating Iroquois and Apache. *"I wonder why there was never a road made between these two cities. Even years ago, when we walked the streets of Iroquois, the city stopped dead. There was never an entrance, or an exit to that place. They've always been separated by this dried barren land."* Olivia thinks over this critical link. *"Why weren't they ever joined?"* She ponders as she steps over and around dried thickets. The occasional drought tolerant green plant greets her with a verdant odor as heat billows off the dusty desert floor. The remains of the sun disappear behind the shadowy outline of Apache, bringing the land into darkness, the stars illuminating the desolate lands around her.

The night air cools her skin and arrests the perspiration from her brow, enabling her to lengthen her stride. Memories come flooding back in the empty night. Mild confusion is common with post rift experiences, followed by a flood of heart wrenching memories, eventually devolving into remembering what she was doing the exact moment before rifting to the past or future. Memories of her youth, her parents, Maria and Jensen; visiting the church and surviving the shootout all come flooding back. None of these to alter Olivia's constant thought of carrying out retribution against Jensen. She freezes as her stomach turns itself into knots. Olivia has always felt the problem with time rifting is the initial period of not being able to remember the time period in the future that you visit. Unfortunately for her, that all changed, as her thoughts turn to a little baby girl, blond hair and striking blue eyes.

"Andromeda." The name rolls right off her tongue, and disappears into the night, along with her happiness. Panicking, the memory of when she and Jensen rifted to the future engulfs her. Their daughter, the young girl whom she encountered in Iroquois, is now missing, and it's all her fault. Olivia fights a dry heave. She's consumed with a sickness that she may have caused the death of her own daughter.

"Oh, no..." She cries out into the night. The memory of Andromeda as a baby quickly fades and now Olivia remembers she must meet her parents somewhere. She shakes off her momentary sadness as she runs through the badlands.

The soft dirt flies in the air as sweat streams down her face, pooling in her shirt. The faint glow emanating from the city of Apache grows brighter with each hurried stride. Olivia analyzes the city, making vain attempts to not trip over the crackling vegetation hidden by the midnight sky.

"I'll have to make it through an alley way and back down the street towards my old house."

Instructions from her mother come vividly back to her, as if she had received them that morning. Olivia wipes the sweat from her face slowing as the outlines of the skyscrapers begin to loom hundreds of feet. The badlands slowly reveal themselves in the expanding light.

Ambrose James instituted the curfew on Apache, due to some rumors of an uprising amongst the citizens who had grown discontent with the

203

constant flow of their tax money into the Department of Time Justice. There were also rumors that one of Ambrose's primary funders for his election years ago was the much maligned Wayne Clayton. One of the local news agencies had run a piece on him and the disturbing safety policies he had employed at Latentech decades ago, when the company was still based in the growing city of Iroquois.

Olivia didn't have any leads to the accuracy of any of those rumors, but she had grown frustrated with the immense size of the Warp Sheriff corps, as well as their unfettered access to controversial weapons programs. However, any action on her end would have endangered her parents' new positions working for the Apache City Council. Olivia pauses in an alley and watches the city street from the shadows. Not a soul is on the street and the only hover car that zips by bears the markings of the Department of Time Justice.

She slinks out across some main streets, concealing her travel in the heart of the city. As she winds her way away from the cutting edge downtown area with sprawling skyscrapers and elaborate technological devices like holographic bus stops, solar powered sidewalks, and the luxurious apartment buildings, she begins to encounter average domiciles, rundown streets, and seemingly forgotten neighborhoods. Most would call this part of Apache ghetto, but Olivia remembers it as her home. Many still inhabit this area of Apache solely out of the reason of affordability.

Olivia courses her way down familiar streets passing her schools, taking a long look down the street where Jensen James grew up. The house still had pieces of tattered police caution tape hanging from it. Nobody had been in that house since the discovery of Miranda's grizzly murder. Ambrose had never gone back, and when he became Mayor he ensured that it was properly guarded and kept from public access. This led to rumors that Ambrose had killed his own wife and didn't want evidence to be discovered.

Olivia sighs and proceeds across the street, cutting over a small hill that years ago had been full of knee length grass, which safely leads into her old neighborhood. Her childhood house has been rebuilt since the days of the shootout. Olivia hadn't been back to it since her and Jensen escaped the initial onslaught of Ambrose and his goons.

The exterior of the house remained unchanged, looking like it did years ago when she was jumping off the roof and running from a brutal gunfight. That night led her all the way back to this one. She was preparing to see her parents for the first time since then, well at least in this modern time period.

She had encountered her parents many times in her travels with Jensen. Some in the past and some in the future, but those encounters were always fueled by some sort of danger; specifically remember hiding behind Jensen's trench coat in a rain of gunfire waiting to die.

In all her travels she had never been hurt or killed, but she still didn't feel bad about turning her back on him. After all, family was the most important thing, and that was something she had never understood as a young girl. The front door flies open before she can knock; her parents stand in the doorway. The trio exchanges awkward half smiles.

"Olivia," Anna clasps her hand rushing forward wrapping her arms around Olivia. Olivia stands there accepting the hug.

"Come on in. We can catch up later, but we called you here for some business." Edmund motions Olivia inside as Edmund peers out the doorway, nodding to a figure in the distance. He shuts and latches the door as he follows the women into the living room. Olivia sits on the edge of the couch, poised to run, while her parents stand whispering between one another.

"So, what the fuck am I doing here that you two couldn't take the time to see how I was doing first?" Olivia interjects, interrupting the whispering session. Anna is immediately reminded of Olivia's teen years.

"Ok, ok, relax honey. I'll cut right to the chase. We need help stopping Ambrose James." Anna sits next to Olivia placing her hand on her knee. Olivia sits back.

"Holy fuck, are you kidding me? So you brought me here, to help you two conspire against the Mayor of Apache. Why? Are you guys still upset over him being a better scientist and making millions of dollars more than you, oh and becoming the Mayor of Apache and guiding into the fastest growing city in the wastelands?" Anna and

Edmund, stunned had forgotten how quick-witted and vile Olivia could be.

"I don't have time to explain all the fucking details you traitorous bitch. Jensen got away and he was going to be our leverage to trade to Ambrose so he can stop wasting money on that foolish charade. You let him get away. We gave you all the information to time rift to and you fucked it up. So now, you owe us. Wayne Clayton and Latentech have some damning information against Ambrose, and since we can't stop him civilly we're going to stop him this way. Edmund leans forward, his face right into Olivia's. "Clayton is bad news too. I saw what he did in Iroquois." Olivia pauses as Anna stands up turning towards her daughter.

"Olivia, we're in a bind, Clayton will have our heads if we don't deliver Jensen or Ambrose to him. He's hell bent on undoing, and stopping all the time travel from ever occurring. We actually think this is a really good idea." Anna walks out of the living room motioning at Edmund to follow her. They leave Olivia with her thoughts.

Olivia wonders if no one in Apache is capable of telling the truth. *"Could Clayton be trying to undo everything he funded Ambrose for? Sure. Could he be lying? Yes. Can she trust that Edmund and Anna, her own parents, aren't actually out for blood and are being conned into helping Clayton? Maybe."* Unsettled, she traces through all the possibilities. The last time she sat with her parents, they had convinced her to turn on Jensen in an attempt to smooth things over with Ambrose because he wanted her parents dead, or at least that's what she was told. Now she's here again, with the same decision to be made. Olivia can't shake the feeling that the last decision she made was wrong, she still longed for him. She sighed, pushing herself off the couch with frustration, walking into the kitchen.

Edmund and Anna stop mid-conversation, and look at their daughter who eyes them with contempt.

"Alright, this is the last time. Tell me where I have to be and what time. I'll be there." She moves up to the side of the island counter. Her parents let Olivia in on a plan involving the old abandoned Latentech research campus, giving her the task of making sure she is in the atrium before Ambrose to watch him. Planning over, she nods and speeds out of the house.

"Olivia, don't you want to stay here and tell us how things have been?" Anna runs, shouting after Olivia.

"I don't think so Mom, you've never cared before and after tomorrow, I'll make sure neither of us pretends to care again." Olivia's words stab Anna like daggers, slamming the front door of the old Jima house behind her.

Chapter 23

Ambrose James hurries down the hallway of the abandoned Latentech research campus. He hasn't been here in over a decade. The last scientific research program closed down when he started his run towards Mayor. Paranoid, he glances over his shoulder He shouldn't be here, but he has to look into something, something that's been troubling him for a few years. He doesn't want to run the risk of being seen here, it wouldn't be a good move for the Mayor of Apache to be seen in the ruins of a company that was wrought with controversy.

A moldy stench promulgated itself in the halls. Ambrose hurries down the final long hallway and encounters two wooden doors with fine brushed satin handles with rather thick chain and padlock.

"Shit." Ambrose wasn't expecting a hassle to gain entry to the old atrium office of Wayne Clayton. As he looks for another way, he notices the drop ceiling tiles above. Rushing to an old conference room, he grabs a chair from around the table and wheels it to rest against the doors. Standing on the chair reaching up to move one of the tiles, his knees wobble as the chair wobbles slightly on its wheels beneath him. Ambrose raises his head into the ceiling looking towards the doorframe, noticing into a small metal cross beam that looks like he will be able to slink over into the atrium. He pulls himself onto the thin metal beam; as it creaks and moans under his weight. He slides the ceiling tile back into place.

Ambrose drops out of the ceiling on the opposite side of the doors, his knees and hands catch him as he falls forward.

"Damn it." Ambrose gets up, rubbing the soreness away. The atrium is eerily unchanged since the last time. He can still remember sitting across the table from Wayne Clayton and signing his life away to Latentech. Undeterred, he rushes between the narrow bookcases that once housed books and trophies, barren now except for thousands of dust particles clumped together in mounds. He reaches the glass desk abandoned, except for empty Styrofoam tray, along with piles of trash at the rear of the atrium.

"Someone's here." Ambrose glances around, making a quick check of the immediate area surrounding the desk. *"Nothing."* He breathes a sigh of relief and moves to the chair behind the desk. Ambrose tugs on the locked drawers to the desk.

He browses for something to break the glass, moving down the rows of bookcases when he hears shuffling back by desk. Swallowing the lump in his throat, he creeps back to the center of the atrium.

A young, blond-haired woman crouches down behind the desk, struggling with the same drawers that had perplexed Ambrose. Trying to crack the doors, she smacks it with her hand out of frustration. Ambrose watches silently, trying to place the familiar girl. When she looks up, he can see her hands are cuffed together and a long thin chain attached to one of her ankles. Before he can return, she shuffles off in a secluded corner of the atrium. Ambrose shakes his head and returns, having not found an item to smash the desk.

"I saw you already. You might as well come out from over there. Why are you trying to get into this desk?" Ambrose questions, trying to draw the young woman out from her corner of the atrium. He watches her chain move as she tries to hide herself from view.

"Hey, it's okay. I'm not going to hurt you. Come on out here, maybe we can help each other?" Ambrose says softly, moving to the other side of the desk, closer to the young woman.

She stares, frozen, hoping that he doesn't actually see her in the unlit corner of another abandoned group of bookcases. She watches him sit on the edge of the desk motioning for her to come out. He looks like a man in one of the pictures she's seen. She looks down at the chain around her ankle, biting her lip as she contemplates moving towards him. She looks back; his hands are crossed carefully sitting in his lap.

"Don't hurt me, I'm coming out there." She stutters weakly. Ambrose stands, wiping his hands on his pants. The young woman slowly slides around the far bookcase keeping her gaze locked onto him. Her blond hair, blue eyes and softened pale skin sinks into Ambrose. He swallows uncomfortably; he knows exactly who she is.

The young woman is a bit dirty and her blond hair is unkempt and tangled. Still, her beauty shines through. Carefully he approaches the young woman.

"I know who you are." He whispers as he draws closer to her. She stops the man that was approaching her was becoming scarily familiar to her.

"Don't worry. I'm not going to hurt you. I saved your life a long time ago and I'm going to do the same thing." Ambrose stops, letting the girl look him over cautiously. She brushes her hair from her face.

"How do you know me stranger?" She stands rigid mere feet from Ambrose.

"Andromeda. My name is Ambrose James. I took you to safety in Iroquois. This is going to sound very hard to believe but I traveled through time to save you. I need to know how you got here." Ambrose takes a short step forward as Andromeda's mind surges with memories. She grabs her shoulder; her scar from her gunshot wound flaring as she remembers the past.

"I, I remember living alone, and I remember Jensen and Olivia coming and promising to take me to safety." A tear escapes as Ambrose rushes up to her.

"Something happened, you were supposed to be safe there but something in the past changed that I couldn't control. That's how you got hurt. Jensen is your father, I promised him in the future that I would keep you safe, but something must have gone wrong." Andromeda leans her head against Ambrose's shoulder.

"I can tell you exactly what went wrong." Wayne Clayton's voice booms through the atrium.

Ambrose looks up, fear coursing through his veins. Andromeda turns, recognizing the old man as the one who carried her away from Iroquois to this imprisoned existence inside the atrium. She slinks behind Ambrose, positioning themselves on the other side of the desk. Clayton steps forward heavily placing his hands on his waist.

"What are you doing here my boy?" He asks, spitting a sickening black mass from his mouth to the carpet. Drips of the black residue drip to the sides of his mouth He slides his thumbs inside his belt, his gut pushes it to strain, tapping his fingers along his thighs. Horrified, Ambrose looks between Andromeda and Clayton; unable to muster up the courage to answer the intimidating old man. Clayton lets out a deep sign and stares at the ground, taking an eternity to speak about.

"I'm going to ask you one more time my boy. What are you doing here?" He projects another thick black blob of yuck onto the carpet. Ambrose swallows a dry lump in his throat; he exhales deeply, trying to calm his nerves.

"I don't think he's going to answer you today." Andromeda steps forward. Clayton chuckles, and shakes his head in disbelief. He slides his hand around his back bringing it forward slowly, aiming a silver Beretta at Andromeda.

"Well sweetheart, he's going to have to answer my question, or I'm going to have to kill you." He pauses to look at Ambrose. "It's your choice my boy. Tell me what you're doing here or watch your granddaughter die." Andromeda's jaw drops and stares up at Ambrose in awe.

"I, I was going to tell you who I was, but I didn't know how you got here. You weren't ever supposed to get found in Iroquois. Andromeda, I'm so sorry. I made a promise to your parents and I've failed them severely." Ambrose tears up, realizing he failed his son and his granddaughter. His apology is short lived as a man with slick black hair and a pencil thin mustache rushes in from another side and a strikingly beautiful older woman strolls in from across the way.

"Anna? Edmund? What are you two doing here?" Ambrose manages to stutter. Edmund shoots a smile at Mr. Clayton.

"Well Ambrose, every now and then someone may get presented an opportunity to be a science rock star in order to hide the real meaning of a company's motives." Edmund's smile fades as he draws a black Beretta from his hip. Anna stands on the opposite side; closer to Andromeda than Ambrose. Anna slides a small white handled revolver into her hand, placing the barrel at the base of Andromeda's skull.

"You're such a beautiful young woman. It's a shame we never got to meet our granddaughter." Andromeda, confused, tries to move her head away from the barrel of the revolver, but Anna mimics her movement, ensuring the barrel doesn't break contact.

Wayne Clayton moves towards Ambrose stopping on the opposite side of the glass desk. "I'm willing to bet you came down here to find our contract or the flash drive that has your initial research on it. You should have just asked me. I would have told you that I destroyed it after you gave me access to it over ten years ago. I never needed you Ambrose; I just needed your research. I knew a few years ago you were trying to get to Jensen so you could keep him safe and tell him how everything happened. Unfortunately, we can't let him find out now can we?" Clayton draws his weapon, shifting it at Ambrose.

"Help us Edmund." Ambrose pleads to Edmund, dropping to his knees. Edmund shakes his head and places the barrel of his black Beretta square to Ambrose's forehead.

"You don't know how hard it's been. I've had to convince you I was helping you protect your son, but convince your son I was trying to kill him initially. Then you complicated things even further and I had to pretend to ally myself with Jensen in an effort to help him take you out. I should have just killed you and Jensen." Edmund presses the barrel harder into Ambrose's forehead.

"Why?" Ambrose squeaked

"Oh Ambrose, you had to have known that we wouldn't take you selling your research to Latentech lying down. We were friends and partners, and you sold out to abandon us." Anna interjects as Ambrose shakes his head in disgust and sickening disbelief.

Edmund lifts the barrel off Ambrose's forehead as Clayton walks over to trade spots. Clayton lines his barrel up to Ambrose's temple, pressing firmly. Ambrose leans away as the pressure increases. Anna pushes Andromeda over next to Ambrose, striking her behind the knees with a swift kick, forcing her to her knees. Anna and Edmund sight their barrels in on Andromeda, while Clayton towers above Ambrose.

"The worse mistake I ever made was that I thought you would do whatever I told you to do. It's too bad your bitch of a wife kept snooping and getting in my way from truly making you great. You could have had everything you could have ever dreamed of, but now Anna and Edmund are going to benefit from your insolent attempts at derailing my plans. I'm going to start with you two and then I'm going to finish what you were trying to take care of. No more Jensen. I will finally be able to go back and alter history, and control every aspect of the future." Clayton grabs Ambrose's hair speaking, slapping the back of Ambrose's head.

"I should have just stolen your research like I had wanted to do. There wouldn't have been decades of games of lying and treachery. I'm going to solve my Ambrose James problem forever." Clayton pushes Ambrose's head down, placing the muzzle of his silver Beretta back at his temple.

A set of red eyes peers through the bookcases, watching the events in the atrium unfold. Her hand slides down to a black recorder, depressing the red record button, with a nearly inaudible click. She slides back away from the bookcases leaving the atrium through a covered hole in one of the glass walls. She sprints off down the side of the abandoned Latentech building, her dark leather boots slapping heavily against the ground. She disappears off the campus and out into the hustling city of Apache. Her stomach sinks momentarily as

216

two faint pops echo behind her, before she resumes her run into Apache.

Chapter 24

Jensen James stands in front of his bathroom mirror; his face covered in dried blood, feeling like he was in a pretty serious fist fight. His mind is racing with memories of Olivia and Andromeda, as he tries to remember everything, knowing there is a much bigger task ahead.

Jensen washes the blood from his face, filling the sink with a faint crimson hue before circling its exit. Toweling off, he walks into the kitchen of the dimly lit apartment. Everything feels familiar; he knows he's been in this dark, rundown apartment before.

Jensen immediately looks down at the floor in the kitchen; the puddle of mysterious red substance is still there, spilling from the refrigerator. Jensen attempts to pull open the door; it sticks as the dried portion clinches the door. Jensen pulls firmer; the liquid caked on the fridge cracks and separates against its will.

A cracked bottle sits upright; the red liquid has gelled on the side of the bottle and through the rest of the fridge. Suspended inside the bottle is a rolled up piece of paper. When Jensen pulls the bottle out, the gel secures it to his hand. Jensen examines the bottle closely; he tastes the liquid. He scowls at the bitter taste. He shakes his hand in an attempt to drop the bottle, it doesn't move from its glue-like state. Jensen looks around for a moment and then back at his hand. He grips the neck of the bottle and smashed it on the nearby kitchen counter. Most of the bottle shatters. The red gel sticks to the counter holding the piece of paper in its suspended state. Jensen looks at the rest of the bottle still stuck to his hand; shaking his head in disbelief. He takes his hand and slides it down the counter, catching the bottle against the marble surface allowing him to free his hand. The goo stays matted against his palm.

Jensen digs the rolled piece of paper out gel and carefully unrolls it on the counter. The ink has started to bleed and fade, but he can make out the message.

Jensen James,

I have your daughter here, from the future. Come find me so we can talk.

Big C

Perplexed, he isn't aware of anyone named Big C, but the name that's in his head, *Andromeda*; he knows she must be the reference of this note. Some of the details of the young girl are hazy, but he can clearly see her full name back in his mind; *Andromeda James Clayton.*

Jensen stands over the red goo, pondering who Big C could possibly be. After he washes off the red goo as best he can, he moves into the living room. He stands there, trying to process and sort all the bits of information all from differing time rifts. He's interrupted by frantic knocking at the door of the rundown apartment.

Jensen freezes as the knocking subsides. He shakes his head, thinking the cause of the commotion has left. He sits down on the dilapidated couch, his head resting back on the padded backing. His eyes close and the frantic knocking returns, louder and urgently. He catapults himself off the cushion.

"Alright, alright. I'm coming just hold on." He yells, as he slides one revolver into his hand making sure it's at the ready. Jensen carefully unlatches the locks on the door; prepared to face whatever, whoever is clanging from the outside. Jensen pulls the door inward and locks his revolver into both hands. His eyes run down the sight and stare right into the iridescent red irises of Olivia Jima. They both gulp, as they stand there awaiting the other to say or do something.

"We need to talk." Olivia finally breaks the silence. Jensen nods, keeping the revolver locked on her.

"I hope you are comfortable talking with a gun pointed inches from your face, because that's about the only nicety I can afford you right now." He shifts his hands slightly, motioning Olivia inside the apartment. She sits on the edge of the couch, and reaches inside her jacket for the recorder.

"Whoa there traitor, I don't think I like what you're doing." Jensen's interruption freezes Olivia.

"It's a voice recorder. I need you to hear what is recorded on here. I have a lot of things to talk to you about, but this is the most important. It's about Andromeda." Jensen swallows, his mouth is parching. He lowers his revolver and slides it into its holster. *"Alright, hurry up with it."* He slides the latch, locking Olivia in the apartment with him. She slides the recorder out and begins to let it play.

She sits on the sofa as the recording device plays back everything from the Latentech atrium.

Jensen stands opposite of her staring down at the recording device playing on the coffee table.

"What is this?" Jensen points at the recording device, starting at Olivia with heated intensity.

"It's exactly what it sounds like. That's Ambrose and Andromeda being interrogated by Wayne Clayton, and..." Olivia pauses and rubs her hands together. "My parents, they've been working together this whole time Jensen. Your father was just a pawn in their scheme and, I, they, years ago they..." She pauses again.

"They what?" Jensen asked impatiently.

"They convinced me to turn on you. They had me convinced that you were irrational and that Ambrose was irrational. They convinced me you two were hell bent on each other's destruction, but you weren't. Ambrose wasn't. Oh God. He wasn't." Olivia sobs, face in her hands. Jensen runs his hand through his hair trying to understand the atomic bomb of information that has just exploded in his face.

"Olivia, what do you mean he wasn't? He wasn't what? I don't understand." Jensen speaks firmly moving closer.

"He wasn't trying to kill you Jensen. This entire time he was trying to keep you safe. He was. Jensen, I think Ambrose and Andromeda are dead." Olivia rubs her eyes, wiping away her tears. Jensen steps back, placing both hands on the back of his head.

"What makes you say that? They sound perfectly fine on the recording." Jensen frustrated, pulls on his hair.

"I heard two faint pops as I ran out of the atrium. They sounded like gunshots. When I left, Clayton and my parents had their weapons drawn and pressed into Ambrose and Andromeda." Makeup smeared, Olivia looks at Jensen who drops to one knee in front of her.

"Do I trust her?" He thinks. Olivia states, hoping he can see the pain of betrayal in her soul. Jensen's slate grey eyes lock onto Olivia's, drifting through their memories, both good and bad.

"Can I trust you?" Jensen asked, breaking the silence.

"I want you to trust me, but I would understand if you feel like this is something you need to take care of on your own. I will stay back or disappear if that's what you feel is best, but I'm wanting you to know, after everything I've found out, that I'm here to help you." She turns her face, trying to hide another tear coursing its way down her cheek. Jensen sits on his knees.

"I'm going to need your help. I need you to go back to the atrium and keep an eye on Clayton and your parents. If Ambrose and Andromeda are in fact dead, then I won't need a rescue plan. I have to go take care of something else before I can confront Clayton." Jensen slides a small, blue circuit board towards Olivia. "Do you remember how to use the holographic communication units?" Olivia nods, wiping her face dry. "Good, that's how we're going to keep in touch from now on. Go back to the atrium and keep me updated with everything that's going on over there. I'll be over there later. I have to

222

go talk to someone first." Jensen pats Olivia on the knee.

She stands and they are the closest they've been since she turned on him years ago. The tension is still palpable between them. Jensen guides Olivia to the front door. Olivia turns as she exits the apartment, hoping Jensen will say something. He refuses to look at her, keeping his feelings at bay. Jensen locks the apartment behind them as he heads towards the outskirts of Apache and she goes back to the old abandoned Latentech Research campus.

Alone on the streets on Apache, she runs back towards the research campus, her thoughts crowded with Ambrose and Andromeda, to her parent's ultimate betrayal, to her feelings for Jensen. She reminds herself that she can sort the latter out later, and to focus on the two innocent people haven't been killed by her own parents, She makes it back to the research campus and creeps along to the hidden entrance of the atrium, making sure no one on the inside can see her.

At the entrance, she checks her jacket and waist belt. Angrily, she realizes she hasn't been carrying her gun all day. She's never left nor done anything without her gun, ever since she turned on Jensen. Now she sits outside a potentially dangerous environment, with Jensen relying on her, and she has no way of defending herself. With a deep breath, she slinks in through the concealed entrance of the atrium.

Olivia freezes, carefully listening for voices or movement from anywhere inside the glass enclosure. She looks through fallen over bookcases and random dispersions of trash trying to see anyone moving around. She crouches and takes low quiet strides making sure to keep up against the rubble and trash to minimize her exposure. It takes her longer this time to get to where she can see the glass desk at the center of the atrium. She watches the area for a few minutes. No one is around.

Olivia moves toward the desk. She can see two small puddles of red seeping into the carpet. She approaches one of the puddles and presses her hand down onto it; blood rises up covering her palm and fingers. Looking around, there is no sign of bullet casings, bodies, or even a trace of Clayton and her parents. Olivia ponders and moves back into the cover of the trash and bookcases, carefully looking around for signs of Edmund and Anna or Mr. Clayton.

"Where could they have gone with two bleeding captives so fast?" This thought dances across her brain. She leans her head back and feels the cold steel of a barrel at the base of her skull.

"Hello Olivia, my darling daughter. Whatever are you doing here?" Olivia's heart fills with fear at her mother's voice. Edmund walks around the front of the bookcase kicking a trash bag out of his way.

"We heard you leave. I'm willing to bet Jensen James is also on his way." An evil smile stretches across her father's face. Olivia closes her eyes as her parents chain her hands together and drag her to the glass desk.

Jensen runs on the outskirts of Apache, towards the old prison. The road that once went out to the prison is long gone, only occasional pieces of asphalt remain, overgrown by the sprawling desert wasteland. Jensen pauses every few minutes to look towards the horizon making sure the outline of the prison is getting closer. The outline has changed in the last years, after years of wind erosion, the seizure of funding, the prison walls have deteriorated and the once massive metal doors have fallen in on themselves. Yet, Jensen is heading towards the prison because he believes there is a man there that will be able to help him. That man's name is Hector Jima.

Chapter 25

A black sedan speeds through the badlands, destined for the prison. Jensen behind the wheel drives the car carefully over the dusty road, wheels kicking up long forgotten dust. As Jensen pulls up to the prison it looks like it has been abandoned for a century and not a decade, a sign that perhaps someone had been trying to speed the process of decay.

Sliding out of the vehicle, Jensen looks around as he places his black Stetson on his head, tipping it slightly over his eyes. He fastens the middle button of his trench coat, loose after all these years but still holds the sides of the trusty coat firm to his torso. He proceeds into the prison, immediately remembering the layout from his rift to save the Jima's and Olivia, a rift he now questions.

Jensen's boots clap against the concrete floor as he slowly makes his way down hallway after hallway, a foul stench growing as he nears the cafeteria where a decade ago, Gus rampaged through an entire squadron of Time Department guards, savagely beating and killing dozens. Jensen pauses at the doors to the cafeteria, his memory of that day haunting him as he peers through the porthole style windows. There is a sea of skeletal remains amongst the thickened, dried blood, its color is as crimson as the day it first flowed, shielded from the harsh sun and elements. Jensen puts his hand on the door, contemplating walking through the sea of death, but stops.

"Rest in peace," he thinks for Gus, and then continues to look for the man known as Hector Luna or Hector Jima. The smell of decay fades only to be replaced by a mix of human feces and rotten food. Gagging slightly, he continues his search through the halls. He discovers a door propped open on the far end of the hallway and makes his way to it, his eyes adjusting as the light from outside the prison becomes brighter.

Jensen examines the door and the lock, noticing the charred marks from where Olivia must have gained access to the prison when they freed her parents. He crouches down, looking for any other signs of use. He runs his hands along the frame of the door and as he rises, he's feels a cold metal barrel against his neck.

"Who are you?" A weak voice cracks out from behind him. Jensen turns slowly to face the long barrel of a shotgun resting on the bridge of his nose, the figure hidden under a hooded robe.

"Don't move. I'll kill you without answers." The voice cracks again.

"My name is Jensen James. I'm here for Hector Jima." The figure shuffles uncomfortably.

"He's dead." The figure retorts.

"I don't think he is. That's why I'm here. I think he's the only one that can help me." Jensen gulps hoping that he doesn't give the figure cause to squeeze the trigger

"Who sent you?" The figure asked restlessly.

"No one, I'm here on my own accord." The shotgun drifts and presses into Jensen's sternum.

"No one has called me Hector Jima in almost twenty years." The figure removed his hood and started at Jensen, who shifts staring up at the taller, larger framed Hector. Jensen was expecting a frail prison, not a carbon copy of Edmund Jima, all the way down the jet black, pencil mustache. Jensen begins to wonder if coming to find Hector is a mistake.

"If you can tell me my real name, I'll spare your life long enough to hear why you are seeking me out." Hector pushes the shotgun deeper into his flesh. Jensen swallowed hard, not knowing if his response is going to end his life and leave him without ever solving the problems surrounding his Wayne Clayton, his father, The Jima's and Olivia, whom his heart now mildly aches for.

"Hector Luna." Jensen said softly, clinching his eyes, waiting to feel a shot rip through his flesh. The shotgun drops as Hector now stares straight at Jensen.

"Alright, it looks like you've earned enough time to tell me your story." He turns and begins walking down the hall, motioning a relieved Jensen to follow.

Hector leads Jensen into an abandoned prison cell with two chairs and a stainless steel table in the middle. A burlap sack is tossed in the corner. Jensen notes the distance to the doorway and the quickest route to hall with the open exit door. Hector points to one of the chairs with the shotgun. Jensen nods and sits on the edge of the chair, carefully scooting it to leave room for a clear escape. Hector slouches down in the other chair, his larger frame spilling uncomfortably around the backing.

"How do you know the Jima's?" Hectors begins, not wasting time.

"I dated Maria Jima. I've been in love with Olivia Jima, and once long ago, Edmund and Anna convinced me that Ambrose James, my own father wanted to kill me. They introduced me to the Awakened, the time rift pills, and kept me safe from my father." Hector sits up straight, placing his gun on the table facing Jensen. Jensen is startled by his reaction; clearly something he said raised concern in Hector.

"Are you an Awakened?" Hector leans in, examining Jensen.

"No, no. I, I don't really even know who or what they are. I've been told a great many things by the Jima's, and Olivia came to me recently which puts a lot of what I've been told into a very different view. That's why I came here. I am hoping you can tell me who has been telling me the truth."

"You're damn idiot. You actually believe that this entire time Ambrose has been trying to kill you?" He shouts pushing away from the table. Jensen scoots back, intimidated by Hector's rage.

"Every time one of Ambrose's goons encountered me, they were trying to kill me. They even tried to kill the Jima's and me in this prison during one of my rifts." Jensen explained confusedly.

"Damn kid. You never thought it was strange that Edmund was leading the goons trying to kill you, every single fucking time?" Hector smacked his balled fist into a wall.

"He saved me at the gunfight in the apartment atrium; if he was against me he would have killed me." Jensen said defensively.

"I'm going to clear this up for you right now. Ambrose James has never wanted you dead. When he discovered his ability to time rift he jumped into the future, he watched the Jima's murder your mother. He spent all those years trying to keep you safe. How much do you remember about the night that you went to the Jima's?" Hector lunges at the table smashing his hands down, staring directly at Jensen. "I was there Jensen. We were there to arrest the Jima's. That's why we took Edmund and Anna; we were imprisoning them to keep you safe. When we got them to the prison, Wayne Clayton and some of the Awakened ambushed us. That's how Edmund was able to switch spots with me. He's been trying to keep you safe for a decade. Where is he now? Why did you come to me and not him? Something's wrong isn't it?" Hector fires a barrage of questions.

"Olivia, she came to me and told me Clayton and the Jima's had Ambrose and Andromeda at gunpoint. I can't trust her; she turned on me during one of our rifts. I sought you out for clarity." Angry and confused, he jumps out of his chair, confronting Hector face to face over the steel table.

The two men stare at each other before Hector frustrated pushes off the table.

"The only way Olivia would violate your trust, is if her parents were trying to convince her that they were in danger from Clayton. It's complete

230

bullshit Jensen. Edmund and Anna have always been working with Wayne Clayton. Why do you think Iroquois was abandoned so quickly? Or did you even not consider that as a problem?" Jensen, who had been desperate for answers, feels sick at this newfound knowledge, wondering whether or not he can trust Hector. Hector throws himself back into his chair.

"Jensen, Latentech was conducted experiments on the citizens of Iroquois when they were trying to develop their time travel. They moved from Iroquois when your father released his discovery. You never questioned the long nights your father worked? Edmund was trying feverishly to get your dad to work with them. He only agreed to go with Clayton when he was convinced that Latentech wasn't testing on citizens. Damn, time rifting as a teenager was the worst thing you could have done. You can't remember anything!" Jensen sits embarrassed as Hector continues to pour out information he vaguely remembers, but never thought to question as his younger self.

"I'm starting to doubt you're the son of scientific genius, I can't believe you've let this get so far out of control. You know your dad's probably dead, you coming here instead of going to help him, he's fucking dead already." Hector fires another insult at Jensen, incensed by the situation since he was unfortunate imprisonment. Jensen shifts uncomfortably, analyzing the small details he's been overlooking throughout his last decade of time travel. Hector shakes his head at Jensen, rising up once more.

"Everyone is in danger the longer they sit on their hands. Ambrose must have discovered the truth in Latentech's past and stood up to him. That's the only thing that I know would cause Clayton to risk people finding out about his involvement with the Jima's and the Awakened. Do you know where they are?" Hector turns away from the confused young man, now slouching back in his chair.

"They're at the abandoned research campus. I sent Olivia back there to keep an eye on what's going on in there. I gave her a holographic chip so she can contact me and warn me if the situation worsens." Jensen slides off his chair moving close to Hector.

"Shit. So not only are two people, probably dead, but you sent Olivia back there. You aren't dealing with humans Jensen. They show no compassion to others. For fuck's sake, Edmund locked me in here for over a decade hoping I would die. My own brother!" Hector walks out of the cell and down the hall toward the center court. Jensen follows him, his stomach in knots, wishing his was at Olivia's side, knowing he will never be able to forgive himself if something happens to her. Jensen fights back the knowledge that that, but he may have just commissioned Clayton and the Jima's to execute his father and his own daughter from the future.

Hector emerges into the courtyard with Jensen. He pauses looking at the old black sedan.

"Hey! It's my old car. I remember pulling this car into your driveway with your dad." Hector spouted excitedly. Jensen mildly confused, remembered the day he found his mother's body, and his dad showing up with a fleet of the black sedans. He tosses Hector the keys.

"You remember how to drive?" Jensen moves to the passenger side of the car, slinking into the seat.

"Nope, but it can't be too hard." Hector plops into the driver seat, starting it roaring to life. Hector tugs the gear selector into reverse and mashes his foot into the accelerator. The tires spin wildly, flinging dust high into the air. Jensen grabs onto the handle above his head as Hector flings the car wildly out of the prison courtyard.

"Just like riding a bike." He smiles, throwing the gear selector in drive and accelerating wildly away from the prison.

The black sedan sprays a rooster tail of dirt and debris behind it as it flies across the old decrepit road. The sedan flies in the air off the small hills as pieces of asphalt shoot off to the side as the heavy sedan squashes down with all its weight, heading towards Apache.

"They're going to see us coming from a mile away. I'm going to fly right through downtown and onto the abandoned campus. They've probably had time to assemble some sort of defense force. I hope you're a good shot." Jensen nods, agreeing with Hector's assumptions.

"I'm decent with my revolvers. It's a shame you forgot your shotgun." Hector growls as realizes he didn't bring a weapon.

"Shut up." He retorts, focusing as the badlands streak by in a blur.

Apache rushes towards them as Hector pushes the accelerator into the floorboard. The motor roars, screaming at its limits as they rush towards the downtown. Hector guides the car between a set of alleys separating a row of skyscrapers as trashcans kick off the front bumper catapulting over the roof of the car. They shoot out of the alleyway blur causing citizens to dive out of the way and a few hover cars to push into each other to avoid a collision.

One of the Time Department's cars engages its red and blue lights and begins pursuing the sedan. The hover car powers its thrusters and maintains a close distance with the older, less advanced car. Hector adjusts the rearview mirror, constantly checking it and the path he's carving through Apache. He glances over at Jensen who drops his window down and slides one of his revolvers into his hand. He cracks the hammer back and aims carefully squeezing the trigger firmly. A single bullet ejects from the barrel. It holds true to Jensen's sight and impacts one of the booster rockets. The small explosion sends the pursuing hover car careening off course and into the side of a building. Jensen lurches back inside right as Hector slips into a narrow alley, the building sides screech along the doors of the car. The car shoots out and across an abandoned street.

Hector rams through a chain link fence as the *Latentech Corporation Keep Out*, sign falls on the windshield. The car barrels down the long sides of the research campus. Hector throws the car into a tight left turn, the tires of the sedan cry out as the

234

car drifts to a stop. Hector and Jensen stare out the windshield and into the glass atrium.

Chapter 26

Jensen and Hector emerge from the car, crouched low beneath the hefty doors, peering occasionally into the atrium to try to see something. Hector leans into the car.

"I see Olivia handcuffed to that desk. No other movement." Jensen nods.

"Same thing, maybe they're already gone." Hector reaches into the car and shoves the gear selector into neutral.

"I'll push; you keep an eye out and shoot anything coming our way." Hector lurches the car forward, pushing, as the heavy sedan starts creeping towards the atrium. Jensen rises and drops every few steps, training his revolver on the atrium. The only thing he can see is Olivia, chained to the desk, who frantically looks behind her, then at the car closing in, shaking her hands violently in the chains as if beckoning them to hurry and free her.

The front bumper of the car comes to rest against the glass wall of the atrium, hidden by the garbage piled against wall. They've made it to this point without any gunfire or confrontation with Wayne Clayton or the Jima's. Hector and Jensen sit behind the car doors looking through the sedan's empty cabin at one another.

"Well I don't have a gun, so you better get cracking. I'll see what I can come up with in the meantime." Jensen nods and slinks around the door. He presses up against the glass allowing the interior wall of refuse to cover him as he looks for an easy way into the atrium. Hector slowly rolls the car

236

back. Bewildered, he watches Hector creep back into the driver seat, roaring the engine of the sedan to life. Hector sits up straight, gripping the steering wheel firmly, gritting his teeth. Jensen scoots down the glass wall, distancing himself between the panel that Hector is fixated on and him.

The tires scream with excitement, billowing large white puffs of smoke as they propel the hefty sedan forward. Hector grimaces as his eyes narrow, focusing onto the single glass plane in front him. He stomps down on brake and accelerator pedal, the sedan lurching forward as the powerful engine begins to overpower the grip of the front brakes. Hector exhales and lifts his foot off the brake.

The sedan jumps forward, the tires leaving hot black streaks of rubber behind them. Hector guides the sedan like a rocket into the glass panel. Dozens of the atrium panels shatter as the bottom explodes around Hector and the car. Olivia jumps on the glass table, narrowly avoiding the black sedan rocketing through the atrium and exiting in a waterfall of glass on the opposite side. Jensen runs in. grabbing her wrists gently and begins examining the chain and cuffs.

"They're locked together, but I'm not tied to the desk. If you can lift up the side legs we can get out of here." She points down at the thick glass legs of the table. Jensen swings to the side and lifts the desk with every ounce of strength, barely budging the table. He looks up, sensing Olivia's worry.

Hector walks up, from the opposite side of the atrium where he just carved another huge opening in the glass wall.

"The chain is stuck around the legs. I can't lift it." Hector shoos Jensen aside, positioning his under the oversized glass tabletop

"Hello Olivia, it's been a long time since I've seen you." Hector casually greeted his niece, who started at him in shocked silence.

"One, two, and here we go." Hector explodes from his squat, lifting the table with sheer brute force. Olivia swings her chains from the legs, as Hector drops the end of the table, the legs crack from the impact. Jensen pats Hector on the back, as he bends to lift the pile of chain off the floor.

"How fast can you move with these chains on?" Jensen asked.

"Not very, but we need to get moving. Clayton and my parents are still here. Ambrose and Andromeda are wounded but still alive. I, I didn't think they would capture me. We have to save them Jensen." Olivia's voice, timid, her eyes beg him for forgiveness.

"We will." Jensen and Hector reply confidently at the same time.

Olivia slinks behind Hector who keeps close to Jensen, but far enough to avoid any exposure to bullets that are likely to start flying their way. Jensen crouches, both of his revolvers drawn, their blue spinning chambers winding with anticipation. The trio treads lightly down the main hall of the research campus, wary at every twist and turn of a prepared ambush by Clayton and the Jima's. Jensen stops periodically identifying drops of blood, most likely from the wounded Ambrose and Andromeda.

There isn't a lot of blood, but Jensen is wary of the blood pattern leading them into a trap.

Buried deep, Jensen's feelings for Olivia begin to creep up. Now he doesn't worry solely about Ambrose and Andromeda, but he now grows to worry for Olivia. Glancing back, he sees her huddled behind Hector, sneaking their way up to where he stands.

"Don't worry boy, she'll be safer back her with me. I promise." Hector proclaimed, shooting a trusting wink to Jensen, who nods slightly.

Jensen leans around another small beam corner, witnessing Edmund and Wayne Clayton dragging two bodies down the hallway.

"They're straight ahead. I'm going to go finish this on my own. Hector, I owe you more than I will ever be able to repay. Please take Olivia back to the car and get her to safety. Olivia." Jensen pats Hector on the shoulder, as he walks around the large man to Olivia. He brushes her hair out of her eyes and looks into her longingly.

"Whatever happens, make sure you live a good life. I would like to be able to live out the rest of mine with you, so if we make it out of here, I promise to love you every minute until our last breaths fleet from our bodies. I love you Olivia Jima." They kiss passionately, and Olivia places her hands on Jensen's as she takes one last long look into his stone grey eyes. Hector tugs on Olivia gently, who turns to run off with him. Pausing, she turns back to Jensen and silently begins "I lov…"

Gunfire erupts into the hallway, as a single bullet flies through Olivia's mouth, slicing through the back of her skull, carrying fragments of her skull and flesh down the hallway. Her soul flees her body instantly as she collapses in a heap. Jensen and Hector dive behind support columns, shielding themselves from the barrage of bullets. Hector glances over at Olivia's lifeless body, coming to grips that he will never know his niece. Jensen's heart explodes in his chest as tears escape from his eyes.

His revolvers sit next to him on the floor, the revolving chambers glowing intensely. Filled with adrenaline and rage, Jensen grabs his revolvers, tossing them into the hall; they float in suspended animation as Jensen rolls into the hallway snagging them. He rushes down the hallway pulling the triggers. The bullets flying at him seem to be floating by, shattering on impact as they strike his trench coat. Jensen runs down the hallways towards the bodies of Ambrose and Andromeda. His bullets fly wildly down the hallway, causing Clayton and Edmund to jump behind similar support columns. Jensen focuses his aim on both support columns as he run, everything seems to be executing in slow motion. He watches each bullet explode from the barrels as they scream towards the cowering Edmund and Clayton. The revolvers begin to transform into a white hot flame; the handles of the guns burning their designs into his palms.

Jensen dives for Andromeda's body, pulling both triggers at Edmund. He watches as the bullets strike Edmund in his center, causing him to drop his Beretta. Landing at the side of Andromeda, he wraps one arm around her, everything blurring in a dust-like wave as they begin to time rift. As their bodies begin to transcend through the rift, Clayton reaches out clamping on to Andromeda's leg. The three figures dissolve in a blur and disappear from the Latentech building.

Hector slinks out from his hiding place, awed by the sudden ceasefire. He looks down at Olivia's body now soiled in blood. Debris from the gunfight is strewn about the hallway. He moves quickly towards Edmund's huddled mass, the thick pool of crimson forming around his brother, looking for Wayne Clayton or Anna, but there is no trace of either. He walks by Edmund who gasps heavily for breath, dying against the column, to Ambrose. Kneeling heavy on one knee, Hector checks for a pulse with his massive hand, but Ambrose is ice cold to the touch.

Kneeling over Ambrose's body, he hangs his head, shamed that had they come earlier, the outcome would be different. He hears Edmund's final, sickly moan and watches as Edmund's eyes roll back into his skull, his chest heaving a final time. Relieved that there is a little less evil in the world, sadness starts to overwhelm as a black boot steps into his view on the opposite side of Ambrose's lifeless carcass. Hector looks up and into the barrel of a gun.

"Ten years was much too long Hector." An eloquent feminine voice greets him. Hector closes his eyes. *BANG!*

THE END

www.ingramcontent.com/pod-product-compliance
Lightning Source LLC
Chambersburg PA
CBHW011459170626
46814CB00008B/2970